O9-CFU-462

SILHOUETTE

SILHOUETTE

A Peacer Novel

DAVE SWAVELY

THOMAS DUNNE BOOKS
ST. MARTIN'S PRESS
NEW YORK

This is a work of fiction. All of the characters, organizations, and events portrayed in this novel are either products of the author's imagination or are used fictitiously.

THOMAS DUNNE BOOKS.
An imprint of St. Martin's Press.

www.thomasdunnebooks.com
www.stmartins.com

ISBN 978-1-250-00149-8 (hardcover)
ISBN 978-1-4668-0267-4 (e-book)

First Edition: November 2012

10 9 8 7 6 5 4 3 2 1

For Jillian,
who may never read it

SILHOUETTE

1

Ironic that I was listening to the Requiem on the night my daughter died. Dark, fiery Mozart that I could feel through my seat—*Hostias* or *Sanctus* by the time the call came.

Lynn and I were in a box at the Carmel Symphony, and as usual I was having difficulty deciding whether to stare at the frenetic strings or swing my chair around to watch the beach and ocean through the transparent back wall. I remember that detail because I missed the first buzz of the glasses in the movement of the chair as I finally turned toward the water. And I know the waves were in front of me when Paul spoke; I could never forget that image and the accompanying thoughts, even if I tried.

The second buzz was unmistakable as I was now sitting still, but I didn't answer right away, because I was hit with an incomparable feeling of surprise and then dread. There were only two or three people who could have been calling me at a time like this, and it had never happened before—hence the surprise. There were very few reasons why someone would use that line, and they were all bad—thus the dread. I could almost feel the same emotions rising within Lynn when she saw me fumbling in my coat pocket for the glasses and slipping them on. Her eyes stayed fixed on me as I raised my hand and touched the top of the right arm to answer the call.

The glasses were on audio-only because I had used them on the drive in, so I watched the spotlighted waves through the clear lenses and said hello.

"Michael," Paul's voice said. "Was Lynette with D tonight?" Then a moment of silence that seemed to last forever. When I remember it, I remember that the waves had stopped moving.

"Wh . . ." My throat constricted involuntarily. "What do you mean, 'was'?" Another long silence, the waves still not moving.

"God." The word was stretched into several short syllables, like he was starting to cry. "There's no easy way to do this. I'm so sorry. . . ." I heard Lynn say, "What?" next to me, barely audible over the din of the orchestra and choir.

"They blew up his car, with him in it," Paul continued. "And whoever else was with him." I jerked to my feet, took a step away from Lynn, and then stopped. Her hand had gripped my jacket. I took it with both of mine and leaned down close to her ear.

"Lynn," as my mind flipped through the options, "just stay here. I'll get back to you." She shook her head, squinting her eyes, and started to say "What?" again. "Just wait here till you hear from me." I said it louder, over the music. I pushed her hand down onto her armrest, as if that could keep her there, and leaped out the door and into the foyer. The big room started spinning when the light hit me, and I changed directions twice before finding the one I wanted.

As I sprinted to the escalator, I heard my name repeated by two voices—the man's was a soft pleading in my head and the woman's was an angry shout from behind me. I started up the escalator, but stopped when obstructed by a wide-eyed couple in tuxedos, who were staring back at me and holding on to their drinks for dear life.

At this point I finally gave attention to the voices. The man's was Paul, speaking to me through the glasses. But I told him to wait, because Lynn had reached the bottom of the escalator and was catching her breath.

"What are you doing?" she said, gasping. Then her anger turned, visibly, to fear. "You're white as a sheet."

"I told you to—" I stumbled backward as the escalator ended, then bit my lip and took her hand when she arrived. As we jogged to the next escalator, I said Paul's name.

"Yes, Michael."

"Just tell me where. I want to talk to Lynn in the car."

"D's city house."

"It's over, right?" I asked, and stepped on another ascending stairway.

"Yes, it's over."

"Are you there?"

"No, but I can be."

"Yes, please. And don't assign anyone."

"Okay. I'll see you there." As I reached up to tap the glasses off, he said, "I'm sorry," again. By then we had climbed the last escalator, and the roof access security booth was in view. Our fast approach startled the rent-a-cop; his hand rested on his gun as I dug the card out of my jacket.

"Any problem, Mr. Ares?" he asked politely.

"No, just open the door." He did, after scanning the card, and we hurried out into the windy ocean air. The Infant was alone on the landing; we got in and took off.

After the beeping and blinking of the air scan stopped, we sat in silence, Lynn staring at me and waiting for me to tell her what she already knew, somehow, as mothers do. When I did, she screamed and slapped at me ferociously until I got control of her hands. Then she just sobbed and kept saying, "It's not true," for the rest of the ride. I said, "We don't know yet," a few times, but it was unconvincing even to me, because somehow I did know, as if I had been there, that my little girl was gone.

The night was clear enough that I could see the castle from far away, as we approached the city. It was unmistakable because of its sheer size, the green-and-black checkerboard pattern of the huge rectangular lightpads on its sides, and, of course, its location. It sat atop Nob Hill, the highest point in the city, protruding thirty stories into the night sky (and almost as wide), like the medieval keep of a feudal lord overlooking the meager dwellings of his vassals. The mammoth structure had lost its wonder for me a long time ago, but on this night, for the first time, I actually resented the sight of it. If I hadn't been working there, of course, my family would never have been at risk.

I steered toward D's house visually, using the big square building as a reference point, and didn't use the windshield map until I was close, and the scan had begun protesting the unusual number of aeros congregated in the air and on the ground near the crime scene. The three or four in the air backed off conspicuously as I approached, much like a crowd of people would do to someone in my predicament. I descended to the street outside D's gate, then locked Lynn's door as she reached to open it.

"You can't just go running in there," I said, and reached for her hand, which she pulled away.

"Don't touch me," she said, then added mercifully, "Right now."

I reached for the belt embedded in the seat behind my waist, and thought about strapping on the boas, as I would if I were working. But I was there as a father, not as an agent of BASS, so I left the guns there and opened the door, freeing Lynn at the same time. She must have gotten the point, because she stayed near her side of the car as Paul appeared out of the small crowd of public servants.

"Michael, Lynn," he said, with a sad but somehow reassuring look on his face. He went to Lynn and hugged her before she could refuse, a gesture that seemed appropriate at first but then quickly turned awkward. So he stepped over to me and took my hand, then my shoulders, in his. There were tears in his eyes—another image I will never forget.

"Listen, Michael," he said. "We can do this as if you were just a civilian. You don't need to know any more than is necessary, and you can let us handle it all. In fact, I would suggest you do that, as Dr. Gross does." He gestured briefly with his head, and I noticed the suit standing at the edge of the crowd, watching us clinically.

"But it's your call, of course," he continued. "Whatever you want."

"I appreciate your concern, Paul," I said to the big man with the wet eyes. "But I'm involved, and I want to know it all. And I want him to be gone." Glancing at the suit.

"Yes, of course," Paul said, and waved his hand at the man, who immediately walked away, muttering something into his glasses. "And Lynn?"

We both looked at her, and she nodded stiffly. The pain on her face made her look like a different woman.

"Then come with me."

Paul walked toward the gate and through the crowd, which parted for us like the aeros had. I stared at his big back, not wanting to see who was there or feel their eyes on me. Soon it was just the three of us and the smoldering piles in the driveway. There were familiar burning smells, plus one that you don't encounter often. I knew what it was, and I was grateful that Lynn did not.

These were the remains of a ground car; I knew that only because I'd seen such things before. For Lynn's sake, Paul explained that it was the one D had used to go back and forth from the castle. His primary residence was in the Napa Valley, on a hill next to ours, but he had kept this place for when he didn't want to make the trip up there. He used the ground car to get here for security purposes, not wanting to attract extra attention with an aero.

I remembered that Paul had criticized D several times for the risks he created even by having the house, let alone by confining himself to the streets by not using one of the flying cars. Paul was repeating this idea now, adding, "That's why we have the damn things."

"Tech been on this?" I interrupted.

"Yes. Garland!" Another regal gesture, and the woman was in front of us.

"Where do you want me to start, sir?" she said to me or Paul, who looked at me.

"Victims," I answered. She looked at Lynn, swallowed hard, and began.

"Darien Anthony, forty-two-year-old African American male, was in the driver's seat, with his foot on the brake. His eight-year-old son, Michael, was behind him, strapped in." She swallowed hard again, but didn't look at anybody. "And on her knees at the back passenger-side window was a four-year-old Caucasian female—"

Fortunately for Garland, she didn't have to finish, because Lynn shrieked and struck at me wildly again. I let her pound away for a few seconds, then Paul and I sandwiched her between us, immobilizing her as gently as we could until she ran out of energy. After an extended silence, her muffled voice asked Paul if he knew where the boy's mother was these days. He said no, and if he didn't know, nobody did. Perhaps she would surface when she heard about it on the news.

I let Paul hold Lynn and turned to the woman again. I asked about the explosives.

"All-switch claymore," she said. "The perp slid it under the passenger side and dove away. The timing had to be impeccable for him to walk away, and the fibers on the driveway are untraceable. He knew what he was doing, and I have some very educated guesses about what else he knew, but I usually save them for when the sim is ready."

"Tell me now," I said, but Paul moved himself and Lynn forward slightly.

"Lynn's had enough," he said. "You need to take care of her. Take her home, let us finish here, and then if you still want to be involved, come in tomorrow. There are no suspects yet; there is nothing else to do tonight."

"I do want to go home," Lynn said, still looking down. "But I want something first."

Paul's eyes started searching the crowd, probably for Dr. Gross, but I said, "Not from those pain parasites." So Paul suggested his father.

"He wanted to see you right away, but he didn't want to impose." He looked down at Lynn, and added that the old man was the closest thing she had to a father. I thought for a moment, then nodded, and joined him in half dragging her to the aero. We made sure she was well strapped, then I lifted the aero away from the street, the scene, the crowd, the fried car, and what was left of my daughter and my best friend. My little Lynn, I called her. My little Lynette . . .

I stabbed at the preset destination screen after I started shaking with sobs, and the aero bore us up the hill toward the castle, the scan beeping at the others nearby. Lynn actually put her left hand on my shoulder at one point, but she didn't keep it there long.

2

When we reached the huge building, the car floated up its side, passing one after another of the lightpads, until it reached the top and landed on the roof. Most of the airborne vehicles owned by BASS entered and exited through the two open-mouth bays in the middle of the north and south sides of the building, but the roof was private access for Saul Rabin's residence. The top floor of the castle was a penthouse apartment, but so much more: an inner sanctum, a holy of holies, a command center, a throne room, and living tomb for the king of San Francisco. And only his three princes—Paul, Darien, and I—could visit him without prior clearance.

I couldn't remember the last time I had landed on the roof—I usually rode the external elevator when I needed to talk to the "Mayor," as Saul was often called. It was always business, of course; I don't think the old man ever received social calls.

He had no friends, after all—just admirers and enemies. Except maybe for Lynn, who was one of the many abandoned children whom Mrs. Rabin had encountered and rescued during her heyday of philanthropy, before the disease had crippled and killed her seven years ago.

Saul's wife had sponsored thousands through her posh Presidio orphanage, but Lynn was the only one Saul ever saw or spoke to, because I met and married her the year after the Mrs. died. The old man had never met Lynn previously, but ever since he'd found out where she had been raised, he had taken an interest in her that was so slight, it would not normally have been noteworthy. It consisted mostly of asking to see her when she visited the castle. But this trickle of affection for Lynn seemed like an avalanche of love when compared to the icy distance between him and everyone else.

Paul landed right behind us and the three of us entered a nearby elevator, inside which a thin red light crawled across our bodies and some hidden hardware confirmed our DNA, brain waves, heart rates, weaponry, and whatever else was necessary to keep the old man safe. I didn't understand much about how the security system worked, but I knew it did. I had been the second man on the scene when one of the tunnel squatters had managed to enter the elevator with an insanely expensive black-market pick, and I had seen the state his body was in after the red line had reappeared on his chest, much thicker and much redder, because the lasers had nearly cut him in half.

No such carnage occurred here, though it would have been a welcome relief from what I was feeling. Instead, after we felt the elevator drop slightly, the door swished open, and as we walked through it to a small anteroom, the slightly different smell and feeling of the artificial atmosphere were evident. Saul was as secretive about the purpose for this as he was about most things; I never knew for sure whether it was a treatment, an immunization, a life-extension technique, or what.

At the other side of the small chamber, another door slid open to reveal our benefactor, standing in the middle of the dark apartment with his huge Chinese bodyguard planted just behind him, as usual. I felt a grave sense of déjà vu, as if I had known from the first day I'd met him that some tragedy like this would eventually befall me, and I would end up standing here before him, feeling wounded and angry, but also guilty for being his accomplice.

"Michael, Lynn," Saul said, the same words Paul had spoken, but the differences reflected the differences between the two men. Paul's younger voice had been musical and soothing; his father's aging one was cracked and ugly. Paul's tone had oozed genuine sincerity; the old man's sounded more like a barked order. Perhaps Saul had seen too much, and carried too much, in his almost eighty years, to be moved by what was happening to us.

I stared at him, wondering about his apparent indifference, studying the thick, lightning-bolt scar stretching from temple to cheek on the right side of his face, and the gang of thinner wrinkles surrounding it. Physically, the older Rabin was similar to the younger, but with gray hair, less muscle, the scar, and a slump in his still-broad shoulders. I also took in the bald, brown mountain of Asian bodyguard behind him, which made the two Rabins' considerable height and bulk seem bantam by comparison. Min never spoke, and seldom seemed to move, let alone show any emotion.

Because I wasn't moving myself, Paul stepped in front of me and relieved me of my usual duty, escorting Lynn closer to the old man so that he could take her hand and contemplate her approvingly. He stared at her for a moment, but didn't wear the customary proud smile this time, and when he said, "I'm sorry . . . both of you," he did sound like he meant it. I also realized that he had called me by my name instead of "Bond," "James," or "007," as he often did, while wearing another small but different kind of smile. I had grown up in England, still had a slight accent, and that character's adventures were reminiscent of mine during the Taiwan crisis.

"My son said you wanted something," Saul said to Lynn, who closed her eyes, exhaled, and nodded. Then she opened her mouth slightly. The old man lifted his hand and placed a tiny disk on the tip of her tongue, which she pressed against the back of her teeth until it dissolved, then swallowed. She asked how long, and he said a few minutes.

"Lynn will need a bed," Saul said to me, then gestured across the big room to a pair of doors. "I have a guest room, if you want to use it. Paul stays there sometimes."

A night in the citadel's dark top floor appealed to me about as much as a room in the jail next door, and Lynn had said she wanted to go home. So I politely declined, thanking my enigmatic employer for his concern.

"You'd better get her to the car then," he said, and gripped her hands tighter as her legs began to wobble slightly. I stepped forward, putting both hands under her elbows from behind, and noticing from the side that a mild smile was tugging at her lips. I pulled her away from the scarred old man, who held on to her hands a little too long. I nodded at him awkwardly, and at Paul, then proceeded to half carry the half-smiling Lynn to the elevator. I got her out onto the roof and into the aero before her legs went out completely, and pointed the sleek vehicle north, toward the Napa Valley.

I retracted the features center and stretched Lynn out so that her head was on my lap, and stroked her hair for a while as the city became smaller behind me and the sporadic clouds above me grew darker, missing the light of the city. *That drug was for me,* I thought, *more than for her*, as I looked down at my recently estranged but now docile wife. I pretended that she would let me touch her like this when she was no longer under the influence.

We had been married for only six years, but reality had already set in. Our initial whirlwind romance had led to a neotraditional wedding ceremony—largely because of the influence of Mrs. Rabin—and then to Lynn's pregnancy during our first year of marriage. Lynn's only mother figure had something to do with our choice to keep the baby, too. Though she did not advertise her beliefs, we knew that she looked with nostalgia upon past cultures where lovers got married and children were considered a blessing. Although at first I had thought the old lady's ideas were rather novel and refreshing, I was now wondering whether her influence had really been a good one.

Thanks to the strain of living together and having a child, our romance had waned considerably. I did feel that Lynn and I were closer friends than ever before, and the happiness Lynette had brought distracted us from the weaknesses in our relationship. But now our little one was gone—leaving just the two of us and a lot of pain to deal with. That pain was tangible right now in the darkness of the aero's interior, as I stopped touching Lynn and stared at her sleeping face, which was enveloped in shadows. My eyes pressed together, and my face screwed up, as I imagined having to face her when she awoke.

She would say it was my fault, of course, because over her periodic protests I had insisted on remaining in my current position, thus putting my family at risk. And she was probably right, judging by the nagging sense of guilt that had been camping inside me since I'd heard of our daughter's death. I had known that something like this could happen as long as I continued to work for this company, yet I had gone on with it anyway. So it seemed that my pain had a name, and that name was the Bay Area Security Service.

BASS was formed in the immediate aftermath of the Great Bay Earthquake, which had caused even worse damage than the one in 1906, which leveled the young city. The security service was the brainchild of then police chief Saul Rabin, who in his illustrious career as a cop had accumulated so much trust and support from the wealthy and powerful that he could pull off one of the most amazing coups de grace in history.

Sociologists, historians, and others who study these things

have long speculated on the dynamics that made this coup unique and unrepeatable. Most of them agree on the "island factor" (or, more accurately, "peninsula factor"): following the disaster, and before the Bay Bridges were rebuilt and the Golden Gate repaired, a psychosocial mass hysteria swelled (some have called it "corporate claustrophobia"), which exacerbated the prejudice in the city among social groups, and especially toward outsiders. Violence erupted in the devastated city, with many of the prominent cases involving people who were not from the city but were now trapped in it. The disaster-relief effort, which was already weak because of U.S. woes at home and abroad, was derailed for weeks by the disorder, until the one thing that everyone wanted was for it to stop, at all costs. The elite were worried about their property, the little people needed the necessities that weren't trickling down fast enough, and the injured, both rich and poor, didn't have time to wait for a "civilized" solution.

The climate was ripe for a benevolent dictator, or a megalomaniacal fascist—anyone with an answer who could make it happen. One man had the opportunity. Fueled by motives locked in his heart, Chief Rabin named himself chief executive officer of this new private corporation, employing unlimited authority with the financial and political support of the richest and most powerful people in the city—plus more than a few jaded billionaires from outside, who found this future legend intriguing. But the most important element of BASS's rise to power, as it turned out, was the annexing of the Silicon Valley and its tech industry, after the damage and chaos from the quake had rendered its security systems useless. When the companies there saw the debilitating collapse of Oakland and other neighbors across the Bay, they begged Saul for protection, and he obliged by making a "covenant" with them (his word) in exchange for exclusive rights to some of the fruits of their research.

CEO Rabin handpicked about a thousand officers from the law enforcement agencies throughout the area, and from the mercenary force of elite soldiers that had been established on Treasure Island in response to the Taiwan crisis and a resurgent China. With the island's fleet of Firehawk helicopters providing mobility for this force, he armed them to the teeth and appointed them judge and jury with a license to kill, if necessary, claiming that this was the only way the city could avoid martial law imposed from the outside. The old man was not creative enough to give these BASS agents a name, but soon everyone was calling them "peacers." This may have evolved from "public servants," a term that he had used for them ("p.s.ers" to "peacers"). Or it may have been lifted from his most famous slogan: "We *will* keep the peace." No one was sure whether the label had originally been meant to convey admiration or cynicism, but it stuck nonetheless. It also struck fear in the hearts of many criminals, who now found themselves in serious danger of losing their freedom, and even their lives, if they failed to change their ways.

Love him or hate him, as many did by now, Saul Rabin had saved San Francisco and the Silicon Valley. Within weeks of the founding of BASS, the only people dying or injured on the streets were the aggressors. The energy that people had been expending on panic was quickly channeled into patriotic enthusiasm for the new regime, and much of the crime that the peacers couldn't prevent was soon squashed by concerned citizens. And the fear of outside intruders, who might rape the limping city, faded completely when the Bay Bridges were reconstructed with airport-tight security checkpoints on the incoming sides, and the Milpitas Wall was erected with similar measures north of San Jose. Residents no longer had to fear that the bloody anarchy in Oakland and the rest of the East Bay would spill over to them.

The government of the United States, weakened by decades of economic crises such as repeated recessions and the payment of debt to China and other nations, was so strained by its attempts to stabilize the East Bay that they were all too glad to grant the city a form of independent statehood that only the most deft politicians understood.

The recent invention of the Sabon antigravity technology and the development of the aeros, however, had turned the young local empire into a growing world power. There were slightly fewer than four hundred of these glorious floating toys, and all were owned by BASS. Saul Rabin was guarding their secrets stubbornly and ferociously, with methods and reasons that were still mostly his own. But as he did, the buying and lobbying power of BASS was increasing exponentially among the nations and corporations of the world. The old man was fast becoming one of the most powerful people on the planet, which was no doubt part of his design. . . .

• • •

As my aero informed me of our approach to Napa Valley and began its descent, I was wondering, as I often did, what use the old man planned to make of his burgeoning influence. I didn't dwell on it very long at this time, however, because I began thinking about the power that I possessed by virtue of being his associate. Working for this company did not seem such a ball and chain anymore, when I thought of the resources that I had at my disposal, and the new authority I now had to use them. As a result of Darien's death, I would inherit his position of tactical command over all BASS agents and operations.

I planned to use those resources, and that power, to find my daughter's killer and make him wish he had never been born.

3

At sunrise I was still sitting on the deck outside our bed-room, the thermal comforter pulled up to the bottom of my ears, securing most of my body from the cool March breezes that swirled more energetically at this height. A few hours before, my nose had started to feel like I was getting a cold, and now my eyes were tired and sore from tears. I had closed them for a couple of hours but had slept very little, alternately remembering Lynette and picturing my hands at the throat of her murderer, who remained faceless at this time.

Lynn had fallen asleep shortly after I dragged her into the house, and as far as I knew, she was still out cold on the bed inside. I had thought a lot about her, too, during the night, wondering if we could survive this. Every path my mind took seemed to lead back to the idea that I would have to leave BASS for us to make it, because in six years I hadn't figured out how to balance my commitment to the company and my relationship with Lynn. And I had finally admitted to myself, somewhere in those dark hours, that there was another reason why my position at BASS was such a sore spot in my conscience, and also in our relationship. I had been dragging my feet for years now in regard to Tara, an Internal Security supervisor at the castle who had been my lover before I met Lynn, and still wanted to be. Tara had told me repeatedly that she was waiting for me to return to her, and to be honest, I had not yet completely disenfranchised her of that notion. In fact, to be perfectly honest, I had actually perpetuated it in many ways. I could rationalize away my guilt in the matter, as I did for most of my night vigil: I had never initiated any contact with her outside the normal course of our work, I had not touched her inappropriately, and the one time I had given in to her pleadings and gone to dinner with her, I'd left before ending up at her apartment. But eventually all those excuses grew tired and weak, and they were pushed out of my mind by the memories of all the times I could have ended it forever, but had not. I supposed that deep down I was still cherishing the memory of Tara and me, and was hesitant to eliminate the possibility of her being there if it didn't work out with Lynn.

Did Lynn know this, somehow? I had not really faced it myself, let alone told her about my inner battles. But our relationship had seemed to grow colder when my thoughts of Tara were more frequent, and that "innocent" evening I had spent with the other woman seemed to mark a turn for the worse in our marriage. Whatever the cause, something had definitely come between Lynn and me, and I couldn't escape the feeling that I had put it there.

As my mind cycled through these thoughts in the morning light, I watched a hawk that had appeared from behind the house and was now circling between me and the spectacle of the Napa Valley, stretched out before me. Our estate sat high on Stag's Leap, a collection of high hills halfway up the valley on the east side. From this deck I could see most of the twenty square miles of estates and vineyards that constituted the largest private, safeguarded community in the world. (At least it had been the largest for a long time—I knew that in recent years many other affluent areas had begun to consolidate, imitating our model.) To my left I saw the distant sprawl of Napa City, twenty square miles of a very different kind of real estate—mostly metal and concrete, inhabited by a very different kind of resident: mostly poor and minority. The air was soupy over that lower end of the valley but clear in the north half, symbolizing the relative qualities of life for the blessed and the not so blessed.

Gazing at the crammed Napa City, I saw the pattern of lines that were sometimes the only thing visible from up here: the elevated freeways running across the city, and the thick belt of electrified metal on the north end that served as a wall between its half-million inhabitants and the estates of the valley. On this somewhat clear morning, I even made out the two breaks in the barrier where the Oak Knoll Gates, East and West, were admitting residents and their friends to the valley, but only after they underwent an ingeniously efficient security check that BASS developers had refined and updated under my supervision.

That had been my first assignment after being hired by the Rabins to bring some outside, objective expertise to their young empire. "Hopefully you will take us to the next level," Saul had said more than once, with his vague, labored smile that seemed to imply a deeper meaning to the words. The old man had broken me in with the simple task of improving the security of the community in which they were generously building me a home. Saul wore that same mischievous smile when he talked about my new house, and I never had figured that out, either.

At the request of its residents and their powerful friends, the Napa Valley had been privatized by our company not long after the quake, the aftermath of which had brought a flood of unwelcome immigrants to the already overcrowded Napa City. Considering the manpower and technical genius at work on the security update, my first challenge was not much of one. But observing firsthand the near impossibility of any undesirables entering the valley by ground or by air gave me a confidence in my home that has endured until this day. I could mourn my daughter all night on my deck with no fear of injury—at least physically.

But now it was dawn, and the time for mourning was over. I forced myself up and out of the chair, stepped through the transteel door to the bedroom, and darkened it for Lynn's sake as I closed it behind me. I had to do all this manually, because she remained unwilling for us to use the Living House voice-command systems that were all the rage in expensive homes like ours. ("When I talk," she said, "I like to talk to *people*.") In the half-light that was left after I had dimmed and closed the door, I saw that she still lay on the bed, motionless. I stepped past her quietly and hit the shower.

After dressing, I leaned down near her face and said something about going into the city, but that I would stay if she needed me. She mumbled, "Go ahead," and shifted to her other side. I thought about kissing her, but thought again, then headed downstairs and out the door to the aero. As it lifted off, I put on the glasses and tapped them until descriptions of my recent messages started scrolling in front of my eyes, but only on the far left side, so I could still see where I was going. I had left the glasses in the room during my nocturnal vigil on the deck, so two calls from Paul had gone unanswered. I played them.

"Michael, it's about four thirty. The techs are not finished yet, so I was going to tell you to relax and get some sleep. But maybe you are. I'll let you know when they're done."

And the second one: "It's ten to six. The sim is done. I'll be here whenever you're ready."

After I tapped the sound off, I noticed the Level Two message flashing below Paul's, so I brought up the details. The caller ID said "Hellboy," and I knew that was one of Harris's pet names. I was shocked, because this was only the second time in several years that he had gotten through to any of us. No doubt he and his lackeys had tried many times—in fact, they probably sent hundreds of messages every day in perpetual loops—but none of those calls had ever made it past the lower levels of Net security. This one, however, like the one about a year ago, had somehow managed to swim a sea of information and emerge on the other side. It wouldn't have buzzed me directly, of course, because Level Two merely recorded the mail it permitted. But here it blinked, beckoning me to open it. I did open it—just the audio—only because I would be in the air for a while and was willing to be distracted.

"Jeopardy question: How did I do this? Egyptian in the Red Sea. Computer illiterate. You'd never understand if I told you. Don't know which breaker got through, though, so can't repeat, or threepeat, either. So on my knees I beg you, *stay* . . . just a little bit longer." He sang this last part, and not very well, but I left it on anyway.

"This is The Game. Give this Ronin back his job, and you and I, Kent and Heller redux, can play iceberg on that *Titanic* from the inside—or you do the exodus, and we nuke it from orbit. This is the Clash—"Should I Stay or Should I Go?"—but *hear me*, you are neck deep in the Inferno, I mean *the basement,* and I don't mean the Flipper's Funeral album—I mean Dante. Except Reformed, not Roman. NO. WAY. UP. The old man is the Serpent, Beelzebub, Lucifer, the Prince of Darkness, the Beast, Azazel, Palpatine, Hitler, Bush III . . ." Some glitch in the program (sent too many times?) obscured the rest of his list, but the verbal diarrhea soon became coherent again.

"That yellow Goliath monster, always behind him on the filmatelevens, more-machine-now-than-man, kill-you-as-look-at-you. You tell me, Air Jordan, if that isn't Evil Soup, what is? The final Nine Inch Nail for me, ladies, was when he morphed the church. Primitive theistic energies had been flowing through there for a century—the labyrinth, last owned by Peaceniks, Inc., was a conduit, an ark, a server, a Salvation Army for the spiritually homeless. Fuhrer Rabin could never let anything that channels light exist in his black hole. But prayer *is* what you'll need, Mick, when he stops liking you Just the Way You Are [singing again] and morphs your ass into goo. Or maybe he'll do a mind lift, a head hijack, a brain boost, a personality pinch . . . jerk with your neuros and make you into someone he likes.

"And what about your Eve and her seed, man? If you're a family man, I'd leave the badlands for Olympus. They have a witness-protection program Stateside, you know. There was *a park up there. . . .*" He droned on, but after the mention of my family I groped at the glasses, touched the wrong button, and then just tore them off. The mental image of Lynette's face literally hurt my eyes, until I forced them open and saw only the aero's dash and the approaching puddles of the North Bay beyond it.

Years ago, Harris had been an agent of BASS before he quit or was fired—I've never been quite sure of the story—and now he was part media icon, part counterrevolutionary, part crime boss, and, as far as I was concerned, 100 percent freak (despite his considerable talents). He and two other disgruntled ex-peacers had led an invasion and occupation of our Red Tunnel a little over two years ago, blockading themselves inside the delta at its end and rewiring the local generators so that we couldn't turn them off. Within an hour—I am still amazed at that feat—the squatters, as we call them, were broadcasting anti-BASS propaganda in an entertaining format to every medium and market in the Bay Area and beyond.

Because of the immediate mass attention to and interest in Harris's sideshow, we hesitated in implementing our original plan to wipe him off the face of the earth, out of fear that it would make him a martyr. And because the popularity of his shtick has remained and grown, we have been hesitating ever since, leaving him and his band to themselves.

This was Darien's call, but we all agreed that so far the tattooed cyber punk had been more media curiosity than political danger, as evidenced by his bizarre dialect. The repeated references from the history of the popular arts—especially from the twentieth century, which to him and his ilk was the "sacred dawn of modern media"—were partly a result of his total immersion in the old video and audio he interspersed with his "social commentary." But he also received royalties, credited automatically over the Net, whenever he mentioned a company's product on the air. We speculated that this, along with criminal activities during their forays into the city, was the primary source of income for the squatters.

Knowing that the Harris problem was an assumable project that would fall to me, now that Darien was gone, I put the glasses back on and made a note to reevaluate our current policy, after D and my daughter had been avenged.

As my aero approached the castle, I studied it and the buildings around it more than usual, the message from Harris reminding me of their uniqueness. This was another of the elder Rabin's most significant accomplishments, because of its enduring symbolic value—the transformation of Nob Hill, high atop the city, into an imposing base of operations. The remains of the Fairmont Hotel and the Pacific Men's Club building, both ruined by the earthquake, had been leveled to make room for the big building, which consumed that real estate and the land next to it, which was formerly Huntington Park.

The Mayor didn't raze the damaged landmark Grace Cathedral, however, but merely removed its guts and replaced them with the most technologically impressive jail ever built. He repaired the dark Gothic exterior of the cathedral and basically kept it looking the same, to serve as an omen of warning for those contemplating criminal activity. He kept part of the name, too, calling it Grace Confinement Center. In one of his few statements to the media, he had defended this perverse transmogrification of the church by calling it "a needed symbol—this is a time for *action* rather than meditation." And he even defended the seemingly oxymoronic name of the jail by saying, with his trademark smirk, "It *is* grace, because they could be dead, but they're only locked up!"

Finally, the handsome Masonic Lodge on the southwest corner of the summit had been repaired and modified to house offices for all the nonpeacer support staff.

Since the world-class construction team was in full stride at the completion of these projects, the city's new Caesar commissioned them to extend the reach of his palace by burrowing a system of tunnels that provided access to various parts of the city from the underground sections of the hilltop base. By the time they had finished, there were three large tunnels and many more smaller ones snaking out into the city, enabling the peacers and their conveyances to avoid traffic and other hindrances on the surface.

While the Firehawk fleet owned the sky, the tunnel system made BASS forces seem ubiquitous on the ground for the first decade, until the more versatile fleet of aerocars was perfected, and then they really could be anywhere at any time. In recent years the Red Tunnel had been lost to the squatters, of course, but the Green and Blue and some of the small ones were still providing strategic help in various crises.

Paul met me in the side bay where I parked the aero, and we rode the elevator to the lab together.

"Are you *sure* you want to do this?" he asked. "We can put another peacer on it—you pick him—and you can go home and be with Lynn."

"Every time I close my eyes I see my little girl," I answered. "I only know one way to deal with that. Besides, I don't think Lynn wants me around right now."

"I'm sorry, buddy," Paul said, seeming surprised that my great marriage wasn't so great after all. "We'll get the bastard." I noted the mild profanity because the fact that he had used it showed how deeply he felt for me and my loss. He rarely used even the most innocuous epithets in public, because his father wouldn't tolerate it around BASS. The old man was known to explain this idiosyncrasy with a standard spiel about professionalism, intelligence, and distinctiveness, but the word was that his late wife simply didn't like swear words. She had apparently cured him after years of crude cop talk, and now he was inflicting this censure upon the rest of us.

The elevator opened to the massive, bustling floor of the crime lab, and we were soon greeted by Garland, who led us to a holo room and fired up the crime sim.

Soon we were standing in D's driveway, at the same place we had stood the night before, but the car was now intact, and empty. I knew this magic was conjured digitally, by state-of-the-art equipment that had recorded every inch of the wreckage and statistically selected the most viable re-creation path from millions of possible origins and trajectories.

"One more chance to step out of this," Paul whispered in my ear, but I shook my head. He nodded to Garland, who touched a remote she was holding and started the holo. D, his son, and Lynette came out of the house and got into the car, in slow motion. The gate opened slowly behind us, and as it did, a dark figure stepped through it from the street. It was in the shape of a man, but entirely black, like a shadow. The tech explained that this was because they had not been able to discern any characteristics of the killer with any degree of accuracy.

I was beginning to feel sick, but I tried to focus on the woman's voice.

"Notice how Mr. Anthony turns on the belts for himself and his son, but not for Ms. Ares. Or perhaps he turned her restraint off, but either way, she ended up on her knees looking out the window, as you can see." The whole scene froze, and after a moment I stepped cautiously to the left and forward until I could see Lynette's face at the window, looking in my direction. There was a moment of silence, then the tech continued.

"I'm sure I don't even need to say this." She hesitated, looking at me. "But if the re-creation is accurate, then your daughter may have known the perpetrator." I looked at Paul, who raised his eyebrows. I was surprised by this because I had been preoccupied with the simulation of Lynette. "And Mr. Anthony apparently did, too, because watch what happens when the killer approaches." The scene came alive again, and the wraith stepped slowly through me and toward the passenger side of the car.

"Do you see it?" Garland said, as she froze the scene again.

"What?" I snapped at her. She was enjoying her job too much, and not concealing it well enough.

"The window on the front passenger side," she said, walking closer to it and pointing. "It's open a little." She looked at me, still too triumphant for the occasion. "Mr. Anthony was lowering the window when the assailant approached the car."

My mind racing, I said, "Play the rest," and she did. As the window continued slowly down, the simulated Darien leaned over slightly, I suppose to say hello, and the black figure slid something small under the car and leaped away from it.

"Stop!" I barked, and she did. "I get the picture." And it was the picture of my little one in the backseat, too real, that stayed in my mind even after the holo became a room again.

I told them I needed a seat, and took one just outside the room, where techs were hurrying about their business, trying not to look at me.

The sim wasn't infallible, I knew, and Lynette could have assumed that position out of curiosity toward a stranger rather than excitement at seeing someone she knew. But why would D put the window down if a stranger, much less an enemy, was entering his property? That made it likely that it was at least a trusted acquaintance, if not a friend. Who else would they recognize, and yet not fear? We had plenty of enemies who could be suspects, of course, and I had expected the investigation to be complicated by the sheer number of possibilities. But this was the opposite problem. Remembering Paul's words the night before about "no suspects yet," I couldn't think of one at this time.

"How sure are you about the window?" I called back into the room, and Paul and the woman soon appeared out of it.

"Ninety-five percent," she answered.

"Tell me about the ordnance," I said.

"Well, the bad news is, it was a very clever piece, designed to be untraceable. But the good news is, that narrows the list of potential sources and those who could use them."

"Which are?"

"American or foreign intelligence," she said. "Or us."

"Us? You mean BASS?"

"Mm-hm." She nodded. "It could have been purchased by anyone who knows our connections well enough. Heck, it could have been made here." I looked at Paul again, who knitted his eyebrows this time.

"So it could be a peacer or an ex-peacer," he said, stating the obvious, and she nodded and shrugged at the same time.

"But utterly untraceable?" I asked.

"Yes, sorry."

"Thank you, Garland." I said. "Is there a Net room on this floor? I forget."

"Yes, I'll take you to Kim. He'll help you out."

As we started through the floor to the other side, Paul asked me what I had in mind.

"I know or have trained most of the agents D knew," I explained. "So I don't even want to go there except as a last resort. To pursue outside intelligence, I'll need to talk to your father about discussing this with his powerful friends. But right now, I want to start with the ex-employee angle."

"If you don't need me, then," Paul said, "I'll go and talk to the old man, to speed up the process." I said thanks, and he added, "I need to tell him about the possible BASS connection anyway. What are you going to do?"

"Run an inquiry to see who D might have known or talked to lately, and then I might try Harris."

"Harris?" Paul said. "Are you sure it's wise to begin a dialogue with that mooncalf? It could turn out to be a black hole for our comm people."

"I don't *care* at this point, Paul," I snapped, reprimanding him with a look not usually designed for friends.

"I understand. Sorry," he said softly, and turned to go.

"Besides," I added after him, "who else would know more than Harris about disgruntled former employees, working for themselves or others?"

He said, "Right," as he walked away, looking relieved that I wasn't angry with him.

As I watched him go, I thought of the many times as a soldier and as a peacer that I had been in the shoes he was now wearing, trying simultaneously to console and to manage a grieving family member who could come unhinged at any time. Now that I found myself on the other end, I was grateful to have someone who cared about me, and hoped that if and when I lost it, the innocent would not have to suffer along with the guilty.

4

When Garland and I reached the net room, she left me in the care of a little Asian with cyberware attached to his head and neck. He ushered me inside, seated me in the chair with the least paraphernalia growing from it, and said, "It's good to see you again, sir."

"Likewise," I said, though I didn't remember seeing him before.

"What can I do you for?" he said, adding a nervous laugh. People had the strangest ways of relating to a man undergoing tragedy. But I ignored it.

"First, I want to generate a list of all former peacers, or upper-level support staff, who have had any personal contact with Darien Anthony since they left. Use my IDs and access his non-BASS accounts as well, but the results are my eyes only." I dug the glasses out, and said he could send them there, as he situated himself in the chair with the most apparatus.

Kim registered my retinal print, handprint, and external code identification, then linked himself to the BASS mainframe and dived into the Net. His body assumed the rigid stillness that was unique to pros like him who jacked in at a level far deeper than mere entertainment—he was working, not playing—but his mouth moved incessantly, softly but rapidly uttering codes and commands to find what he was looking for. I knew that navigation, download, and other functions could be manipulated by thoughts alone in the newest technology, with the controls taking the form of complicated patterns, such as long words spelled backward, so they wouldn't be accidentally triggered or diverted by random brain activity. But that was cutting edge at this point, and the best techs still used voice recognition, which was faster and more trustworthy for them.

As I watched Kim do his thing, it occurred to me how I might know him. So when he emerged from cyberspace and told me the data I requested would be on my glasses in a few minutes, I made some conversation with him to pass the time.

"You weren't at the Presidio, were you?" I asked.

"Yes; I hoped you'd remember me from the reunion," he said with an eager smile, some sweat from his dive still glistening above it. Following my eyes, he wiped it with his sleeve. "Your wife was there for a few years while I was . . . or I should say, I was there when she was." He chuckled nervously again, equally excited and embarrassed to be talking to an "important person."

There were not too many BASS employees from Mrs.

Rabin's orphanage, especially at this level—someone had to be exceptionally gifted and skilled to succeed here, so favoritism was not very practical. But out of the thousands of children who had lived at the Presidio, some were bound to be prodigies, and the education they received made good use of their abilities. Also, I remembered Saul saying something about how the program produced the kind of ethical character he desired, so perhaps that had given someone like Kim a leg up on the competition.

"I didn't know her personally, just saw her around," he added, then smiled again. "Very beautiful." Now he was even more embarrassed, so I just nodded in agreement and smiled politely. For the next few moments he studied the hardware in front of him, and I studied the hardware attached to his head and neck. I found it somewhat odd that a well-educated man would have surrendered to such implants, or "imps" as they were commonly called, because "cyber virginity" was a mark of status and prestige among the upper crust. Foreign objects in the brain were thought to be a possible gateway to external control, and freedom from them spoke of individuality and personal power. And even though techs like Kim had to be augmented to do their jobs sufficiently, they were inevitably viewed and treated as second-class citizens, with no opportunity for advancement beyond the service professions.

At this point the mainframe informed me politely that the data I asked for had been transferred to my "personal desk." I put the glasses on and pressed the arm a few times until I found the file, then switched to all-video so I could read the fine print underneath the seven names listed there. Displayed within the lenses of the glasses, the script then filled my vision, but seemed to be to be about a foot away from my eyes, so I could read it normally.

One entry was a former high-level tech, a woman, whom D had visited in June of last year. But the record (drawn from the use of security passes, no doubt) showed that he had visited her in a hospital in L.A., and she was dead now. So, although that might have been an interesting story to pursue, it wasn't pertinent to my investigation. I began to feel a bit of voyeuristic guilt for peering into my friend's life this way, but I pressed on anyway.

The next three names on the list were ex-peacers, but none of the contacts was very recent, and D hadn't talked with any of them more than twice. The descriptions of the nodal points surrounding the contacts yielded no clues, either, so after studying them to no avail, I again thought of asking Harris about the names. Even though it had probably just come from hearing his message earlier, I decided to follow the impulse. But I would have to make use of Kim's expertise to prevent any sabotage by the freak. So I put the idea on hold for now and looked at the last three names on the list. They were Saul Rabin, Paul Rabin, and Michael Ares. I asked Kim why, because I had asked for *former* BASS employees.

"Oh, when I was scanning the nodes," he answered, "I saw that Mr. Anthony had twotted about you, and I thought you might want to see what he said . . . I mean, thought. That's why those names are in light blue-green. Speaking of opening your mind up . . ." He gestured like he was taking a lid off his head.

While investigating crimes, we often extracted and looked

at Twotter files, but I was surprised that anything came up with D, because I had presumed he shared the revulsion that I and many others had to the idea of people broadcasting their thoughts on the net. In fact, I could only remember him *agreeing* with my negative references to this pastime, which had started years ago with people typing and speaking their thoughts on Twitter and then progressed to this ultimate form of narcissism with the advent of neural interface (pronounced "twoughter," but spelled the easier way). Kim apparently sensed my bewilderment, and explained.

"He only twotted one time, and for only a few minutes," he said, his body going stiff again as he looked at his files. "And he just sent it to a personal account, not the whole network . . . probably curious to see how it came across. But she never deleted them from her system."

"She?" I asked.

"His last three payments before this were for a high-class escort, a hotel room, and a lot of expensive booze from their room service. Cross-referencing the records from the escort service yields the ID of the woman, and the history of her purchases reveals that she herself did not have implants but owned a pricey external rig, probably one of her prize possessions." He stopped viewing his files and looked over at me. "My guess is they got liquored up, she discovered that he had never used Twotter and talked him into trying the rig. They decided he would think about his job . . . maybe random or maybe she wanted to know more about the inner workings of BASS, while his inhibitions were down. Who wouldn't?"

"So he agreed to send the twots to her private account so he could view them," I said. "And then she didn't erase them . . . maybe because she has that hooker's mindset of saving info for blackmail. In case she got into a desperate situation and needed something to leverage."

"Could be," he said, raising his eyebrows and nodding.

"Can you delete hers while I take a look at our copy?"

"I think so," he said, and at my nod, he dived back into the net.

I tapped and moused my glasses until the text of D's twot appeared, and chose the audio-accompaniment option. Now I *really* felt bad about this voyeuristic trip into my friend's private life, but I also felt compelled to find out his unfettered thinking about the company, and to follow up on the possibility of information pertaining to the case. The Twotter software was designed to filter out completely random, unrelated thoughts and record only those that connected somehow with the previous topic, but it still contained some disorienting parentheses. . . .

Okay, think about my job, think about my job . . . I work for BASS, the BigASS we call it, when we don't like something, not like yours, yours is . . . think about my job, okay, think about . . . BASS is Saul, Saul is BASS, he is amazing legendary iconic, old, scar, my head is itching, do you like this thing?, she can't hear me . . . BASS, Saul is so different from what you would think, would rule this place, he is like an antique in so many ways, I don't mean old, he is old, I mean antiquated with these old ideas, values, and in this place that was so . . . progressive, gay-rights capital and all, does she do women? she can't hear me . . . but progressive, cats laws about cats, pets' rights you name it . . . the only way the Mayor, Rabin, could ever run this city is if it was destroyed, going to be destroyed, he was the only way to stop, no atheists in foxholes, no atheists in an earthquake . . . atheists means no God no religion, he doesn't wear it on his sleeve but it's underneath, down deep, from his generation maybe, no he's not that old, I hope she's not underage, doesn't matter, who's going to arrest me, me? funny . . . I won't arrest me, but why do I feel bad about it . . . Paul's better, he's religious too I think but not . . . intolerant, he doesn't isn't won't judge us, he wouldn't arrest me, Michael is not religious, British not, he's married though, that might be better for Saul, he's not better than me, why does the old man prefer him, because he's white? . . . she's white, I like white, she can't hear me . . . could be a white thing, I don't know, do I really know? white is an old idea too . . . but I shouldn't think this way about him, he's never done anything bad to me, it's his money here, look at this room, look at her, look at her lips, what? . . . keep, your, eyes, closed, oh, okay . . . no, my head itches, I'm done.

There was nothing here pertaining to the murder case, but it was definitely interesting. I'd had no idea that D had suspicions about Saul Rabin, probably because he could never say them in his position, and I was even more surprised that he thought I had been favored by the old man. It sounded like D had found out that Saul was grooming me ahead of him, though I didn't see why that would matter much to him, with Paul as the heir apparent to the throne. When the king eventually passed on, his son the prince would constitute his own court. Also interesting were D's thoughts about the underlying beliefs, more palatable in the son than in the father, which brought my attention back to the Asian tech, who was now finished with his dive and staring at me.

"Did you get rid of her copy?" I asked him.

"It's gone, far as east from west," he answered. "That's from the Bible, you know."

"What?"

"That expression . . . our sins are sent away, as far as east from west."

Riiiight, I thought, realizing that someone had indoctrinated this young man in one of the much-maligned religions that followed an ancient book as if it were true. I wondered if he was of the fringe variety who were hounded by activists because they thought only straight people were going to heaven. That viewpoint was about as popular as an enema with most people, and it could get you killed, because the only thing not tolerated in our culture was any form of intolerance. BASS had taken quite a bit of heat, in fact, because the Mayor had refused to prosecute such religious varieties, as long as they did not commit violence against others. I knew he had many old-fashioned ideas, but I was still a bit surprised that someone like him would be allowed to work here.

"Did you learn that at the Presidio?" I asked.

"Some . . . there were some believers there. More than you might think." He winked, inexplicably. "But I was born and raised in South Korea."

"Ohhh," I said, nodding. Although his kind of fundamentalist faith had been on the decline for some time in North

America, I knew it was still thriving in some other places around the world, especially in that beleaguered Asian country.

"Well, nice work on the file," I said, then exited out of it, reduced the list of names to the far left side of my view, and asked Kim to put a call in to Harris.

"Use a screen, not my glasses," I added. "And try to keep him from lifting any addresses during the call."

"I can't guarantee that," replied the little tech. "There are other rooms in the castle that could do the trick, though." I told him to go ahead and do the best he could.

Less than a minute later, we were both looking at a previously recorded message of a man shown from the waist up, dressed only in dozens of tattoos and a cybernetic eyepiece. As the image of Harris greeted us in his characteristic soundbytese and explained how he could not possibly answer all the calls that came his way, the environments behind him changed every few seconds from beachfront to nightclub to underwater to the Great Wall of China, and so forth. His tattoos also frequently stretched out to display themselves closer to the viewer, illustrating whatever point he was making at the moment and then receding to their home on his skin.

Kim was frantically resetting to retry when a live Harris suddenly appeared on the screen. He was wearing the same tattoos and eyepiece but was now situated only in a room crammed with arrays of equipment pressing in on all sides of him.

"Whoa! Whoa! Whoooooa Nelly," said the man, mashing some buttons in front of him and below the screen. "Is that really you? Sorry, it took me a New York Minute to recognize you. Is this really coming from the Black House, the Bates Mansion, the Tower of Babel? Don't go, Mother Lode, whatever you do. . . ." I waved a finger at Kim, who disconnected in a rush and left the room.

"I'm here, Harris," I said, and he froze, then smiled when he found my face on one of his screens. This was a big moment for him. He began talking like a news anchor.

"Sir Michael David Ares, born Manchester, England, knighted by His Majesty Noel I at the young age of twenty-six in honor of his exemplary service for the New British Empire in the Taiwan crisis. Retired from British military service to accept the position of executive agent with the Bay Area Security Service. Expected to replace the late Darien Anthony as senior executive agent, making him now one of the three most powerful men in the city-state of San Francisco." The news about D had taken only a few hours to reach him, despite no public statements by BASS. Maybe he *would* have some information for me.

"So you *can* talk like a normal person," I said.

"Normal person! Those Talking Heads on the news? I used to be one before my BadASS days, you know, and before my subsequent ascension to godhood. Believe Me Chelsea, they are *not* normal people! By now most of them are constructs, *of course*. Like I'm thinking you are, because Why Oh Why would *Sir Michael Ares* [in the news voice again] call *moi*?"

"Because I want some information, *of course*, and if you give it to me, I might consider letting your sorry arse stay in that hijacked asylum, rather than flushing you out like the sewage you are."

"Oooooo," rolling his head back and forth, "I'd like to see you try. It would be more like Vietnam or the Taurans than that staged cakewalk when you rescued that floating factory. Our West Coast offense is only words, pictures, sounds—but we can stop the run if we have to." He paused to let that sink in. "Buh temee hall ah can hep ya, massa, an ah sees wuh ah cul do."

"You obviously know about Darien Anthony—"

"Was much better on the field than on the front lines of our local media wars."

"Do you know who killed him?"

"How in Sphincter City would I know that!"

"Then do you know if any of these former peacers were anywhere around here last night—Miguel Jimenez, Valeri Korcz, Therese Bester?" Those were the names from the list.

He stared at me for a moment, lost in his thoughts, then he seemed to be struck by one.

"I'll tell you what, girlie-man," he finally said, the last phrase in some sort of foreign accent. "I may be able to scratch your itch, at least *un poco.* But you have to give me a minute. How can I reach you?"

"Don't call me, I'll call you," I said, then added "in one minute," not wanting to spend more time than was absolutely necessary with this long shot.

"Right on," he said, and was gone.

I called for Kim, asked him to forward a recording of the

upcoming conversation to my glasses, and as we waited for the minute to pass, I asked, "Why do you suppose Harris makes those media references on a private call, when he's not broadcasting and getting paid for them?"

"Maybe he is," Kim said. "With his software skills, it wouldn't be hard to cheat his customers. I hear there's some pretty sophisticated cybercrime going on in the Red Tunnel. But then again, maybe it's just second nature for him. You become what you say, right? The word is in your mouth and in your heart."

I didn't know about that, but a minute had passed, so I told him to put another call through and leave again.

Harris seemed genuinely glad that I had called back—perhaps too glad. He was smiling and shaking his head.

"And I thought *I* was good," he said. "Our recording of that powwow we just had looks like the end of *2001: A Space Odyssey* and has no audio, period. I don't suppose you could tell me how your people do that?"

"I have no idea," I said. "Do you have anything of use for me?"

"Believe it or not, Mulder and Scully, I do," he answered, and my back stiffened suddenly. "The truth is out there. It just so happens that Mr. Korcz has been in town for three days, and when he stopped by the establishment of one of our subsidiary business partners, they say he checked some interesting hardware at the door." He reached behind him to turn a dial, stopping some music that had begun to play during his explanation. Then he looked back at me.

"What specifically?" I asked.

"Guns the type that Working Men use, and a couple of hand-size disks that our amigos guessed were some kind of high-tech explosive. That's all they said."

I didn't know if I was more excited to have a lead or shocked that I got it this way.

"You're not asking me for anything," I observed.

He smiled, winked, and said, "No charge," then started singing. "I'm as free as a bird now, and this bird you cannot chayeeyange . . ." I reached for the only button I knew in front of me and turned him off.

Eager to expend the angry energy simmering inside me, and not wanting to waste time wondering about the freak's motives, I made a beeline to the Surveillance Center by way of one vertical and two horizontal elevators. I asked the nameless third-level on duty if she could insert an ex-agent's DNA into the Eye's database, and when I got a positive answer, I told her who and why. Then I took a seat and waited a few minutes for her to return, noticing that many of the other techs had slowed to half speed and were glancing at me inconspicuously. By the time the scan was under way, there was a crowd of them gathered behind me, all watching the ten-foot-wide holo projected from floor to ceiling in front of my seat.

We normally used the Eye to locate and track criminal suspects whose genetic ID had been recorded by us or some other law enforcement arm. But from time to time we needed it to find an agent, so I knew that as long as we still had Korcz's print, and as long as he was still in the area, the Eye could find him. To locate him in another part of the country or world would have taken some finagling with other governments that maintained their own similar satellite systems, but it could be done.

That turned out to be unnecessary, however, because the projector soon displayed a map of the city, with our location highlighted toward the top and a similar blip flashing in the south. The map then began to enlarge, zooming in on the bottom half until a red circle representing Korcz was in the center of the holo. It then abruptly disappeared, replaced by a live aerial shot of Candlestick Park (affectionately known as the Stick), an old sports stadium south of the city that had been destroyed by the quake but then preserved in its ruined form as a popular tourist attraction. The view began to move closer to the wrecked arena, which looked like some massive monster had emerged out of the water next to it and taken a big bite out of its south side, taking some of the ground with it as well. It reminded me of the way the Colosseum in Rome had looked before Pal-Tel made their "statement to the world" with that tactical nuke.

When the Stick had grown to fill the screen, the projector superimposed a series of green dots, and one red one, which were moving around slowly at various locations throughout the large structure.

"We can't get a visual, because he's inside," said the third-level. "But this is thermal." She manipulated a remote, and the view encroached further on the red dot, until it turned into the red shape of a man, and I could see for the first time that he was accompanied by two green shapes, smaller and unremarkable, except that one appeared to be a man and the other a woman. I asked the tech where they were, but she wasn't sure and looked around for some help. One of the onlookers spoke up.

"I think they're just in the tunnels there, where they have those exhibits. You know, the videos and such from the quake. Looks to me like he's just doing the tourist thing. There's nothing else there, that I know of." I looked back at the third-level, who shrugged, then touched her remote again.

"Whatever he's doing, he's armed," she said, pointing to the holo. I looked that way and saw the red figure, now enlarged much further so that I could make out the two small blotches of black on his lower back, near the kidneys. The same place I wore my boas. "But his companions don't seem to be," she added, looking at me to indicate that her job was finished.

"We'll have a little talk with him," I said, and headed for the garage, barking orders into the glasses along the way to form an assault team of three aeros and a falconer.

5

Before noon, my aero, the three others, and a big flying van were approaching the old stadium over the hill just north of it. During the brief journey, I had wondered why Korcz would be hanging around a tourist spot if he had just committed a high-profile murder, and I had been introduced to Twitch, the new head puppeteer for this particular falconer. He told me his nickname had come from his mastery of holo games when he was "younger"—he wasn't old enough yet to say "young." Then he excitedly added, "But that was nothin' like this, no sir." His visual in the corner of my glasses revealed him to be a slight black man, his eyes and ears presently hidden by various contraptions as he and his team prepared to launch and guide the birds by remote control.

I also had taken a call from Paul, who looked like he was troubled and trying to hide it, but not quite succeeding. He asked what I was doing, I told him, and then he tried to talk me into letting someone else handle it. He wanted to talk with me at the Ranch, for some reason, and I guessed this was related to the distress behind his eyes. I told him that I would finish my business here, then call him, and he reluctantly agreed.

"The target is currently stationary," said the third-level back in the Surveillance Center as the Stick came into full view in front of us. I heard her voice in the glasses, which were now open to several channels. "And his accomplices also."

"Good timing," I said, then told the aeros to land and the falconer to launch. Out of the rear of the skyvan sprang three small black shapes, like thick meter-long bullets, which then extended their wings and dived after the descending cars. Each one accompanied a different car to its landing spot, then they hovered behind the agents as they entered the building at three different places.

After directing my aero to hold its position, I turned the glasses to all-video and called up feeds from the Eye and the falconer. They filled my view, looking like a movie screen divided in half. On the left was the Eye's thermal view of the stadium, with Korcz appearing as a red figure, his accomplices as green, and the approaching peacers as blue. The falcons were represented by smaller blue blips. The right half displayed an alternating view from the front cameras of each falcon, until I told Twitch's editor to leave it on point for now.

I set the glasses so that one tap could bring the falcon view to full screen, and tried it. Immediately I was hit by the odd sensation of virtual motion, as I seemed to be floating about five feet behind the point man, following him through a big, curved tunnel inside the stadium where people used to walk to find their seats, buy food and drink from the concessions, and use the bathrooms. A few of the food stands were still food stands, but others had been converted to walk-in exhibits commemorating the various effects of the quake. There were tourists walking the hall and observing the displays—a thin crowd that parted easily when they caught sight of the goggled soldier and the sleek black metal bird moving through them.

"This is a flatmovie-viewing room," said the peacer I was following. I knew it was he because "A-1" appeared in the corner of my glasses while he spoke. He moved over to the wall to his right and drew his gun. The falcon I was looking through swung out and around until it faced a door that said PRESS CLUB THEATER and the park employee standing next to it in his conspicuous uniform. He was dressed like the old popcorn and hot dog vendors who had worked the crowd during sporting events, and he was frozen stiff, staring openmouthed at the menacing black machine.

While the point man gestured with his gun, softly but firmly telling the nervous man to step away from the door, I switched back to the dual screen and took in the thermal. The second peacer was arriving at the other entrance to the theater, farther down the same tunnel, and the third was positioning himself on the other side of the theater. I wondered where this was, so I asked the editor to give me F-3. In a moment, I was looking through another bird at the third peacer, who was outside. He was crouched near a door on the high, thin walkway that had been extended from the elevated press boxes on the intact, north side of the stadium, so that the visitors who were bold enough to traverse it could see the whole inside of the stadium, including the wrecked south side, in all its glory.

"Go full for a second," Twitch said to me, and I did, the falcon's view filling mine. He tilted it down, giving me a vertigo-inducing look over the thin railing, then swept the stadium briefly, reminding me of my one visit here as a tourist, which was quite enough, thank you very much. The stadium's owners had chosen to leave the ruins basically as they lay (fallen light rigs, bloodstains and all) after the quake had rudely interrupted a concert, killing more than two thousand people and wounding more than ten thousand. By a gruesome twist of fate, that particular daytime event was being broadcast live, so numerous cameras with independent power sources captured hundreds of images of people being crushed, impaled, and dissected by falling debris, or thrown to their deaths from the upper levels. The recovered footage was now shown daily to spellbound sightseers in several theaters like the one Korcz was in now.

I reverted to the split screen and told Twitch, in my business voice, to send in F-1. On my right screen, I was back in the first falcon, which floated past the point man and into the door he had opened. At first, the interior was all black, but then Twitch turned on the infrared and I could see, from the side, quite a few people situated in ascending rows, staring at the screen. He turned the falcon to show both agents readied near the two entrances, then flew it to a spot in the air between the screen and the people.

Through the bird's speaker, and in an electronically modified voice that boomed louder than the movie, Twitch told everyone to remain in their seats and be calm. Then he maneuvered to the left middle of the audience, and I saw the small blue blip nearing the red and green ones on my left screen.

"Mr. Valeri Korcz," the hovering falcon said as I switched to full screen so I could have a better view of the man, whose two accomplices turned out to be an elderly couple. "Please put your hands in the air and move slowly to the end of the row. No harm will come to—"

And then all hell broke loose. Korcz dived *behind* his aging friends, and Twitch proved true to his name, firing immediately. The soft shell streaked right between their heads and hit Korcz on the hip, exploding in a cascade of green gas. The old couple, and whoever else was sitting close enough, slumped over, unconscious. But Korcz must have exhaled with impeccable timing (not an easy trick), because through the cloud I saw him disappearing off the screen. Twitch must not have seen it, because he didn't move the bird right away, so I switched back to dual screen and watched the red blip dive for the back right corner of the room. The two peacers, and the second falcon, gave chase as Korcz stepped over seats and gasping people until he finally barreled through the exit, finding himself on the high walkway about fifty feet from the crouching third agent.

The editor put me in the third falcon just in time to see Korcz simultaneously reach for his guns and dive backward—another impressive move. The peacer in front of me fired two stopper rounds, but because of the slight curve in the walkway, his moving target was partially obscured, and both of the soft-steel Xs grazed the railing just enough to be detoured.

What wasn't obscured at all by the railing, however, was Korcz's angle on the hovering falcon, and he earned kudos again by sending a barrage of bullets its way. All I could see through the camera was the flash of his muzzles in the distance, and then darkness, as it became obvious that at least one of the projectiles had smashed the lens. Others must have impacted elsewhere on the bird, because it fell to the walkway, distracting the crouching peacer long enough for Korcz to climb over one of the old press boxes and into the upper-level seating. I gathered this from the thermal view, because the right side of the glasses was dark until the other falcons emerged from the theater and fanned out toward the area where Korcz had disappeared.

"A-2, go back into the tunnel and stay parallel with his location," I said. "There's nowhere to go up there, so we just have to keep him from leaving."

The peacer and his falcon obeyed, heading back through the theater, while the other two men pressed up against the press boxes and moved cautiously forward, waiting for the remaining bird to locate Korcz. It did, not long after, and the man was running wildly through the seats toward the west, away from the agents' position. I watched him from a distance, because Twitch had pulled the falcon way back, not wanting to lose another one of his toys. I soon grew thankful for the wide angle, however, because at its left edge I could now see Korcz's objective.

The mad run was not mere desperation, after all.

I moused the glasses until the falcon's view was reduced to the far left and I could see through the rest. I grabbed both ends of the gun belt embedded in the seat behind me, snapped them together at my stomach, and pulled the holstered boas around to the front. I throttled forward, toward the top of the stadium, and slightly to the left as I gauged where Korcz would be by now.

When the aero crested the top of the old ruin, I saw the tiny shape of the man, running with his back to me, well on his way to the floor of the stadium, where he could escape out the other side. As I presumed, he had been running for one of the stadium's huge light poles, which had fallen across the upper level and been bent, but not broken, its upper length and the lights attached to it stretching all the way down to the field. Korcz was using it like a ramp, running down it with the concentration and steel nerves of a high-wire artist. The two peacers on the catwalk were firing at him, but the stopper rounds weren't very accurate at that distance, and only a few even hit the metal around him. Twitch, taking this all in through his falcon, spoke up.

"D'you want I should make a rush at him and gas him?" he said anxiously.

"No, just hang," I answered. "And tell the castle to send a few more cars, in case this doesn't work."

I was still behind Korcz, but getting closer, and I had lowered the aero down near the rusty metal of the fallen pole. I slowed it slightly, hoping he wouldn't hear the hum until I was upon him, and not wanting to kill him just yet. As he grew larger in the windshield, I brought the car down even farther and pointed the front bumper at his back.

About a car length before I would have hit him, he suddenly looked back and then dropped, bouncing off the pole and down into the remains of the light array resting on the field. I couldn't see whether or not he had lost the guns, so I switched the aero to hover and nudged it to the left a bit. As it was stopping and banking slightly, I slid to the passenger side, lowered the window, drew both of the boas, and stuck them out in front of me as I extended up and over the top of the car. Though my head, shoulders, and arms were exposed to the light array, the rest of me was safe behind the heavy fibersteel of the aero. I scanned the bulky, smashed mess with my eyes and with the guns, squinting at the reflections shining from it. My finger gripped the trigger of the right boa, with its fourteen caseless stopper rounds, but my other one only rested on the guard of the left gun, which held twenty killers.

When nothing stirred in the debris, I retreated slightly into the car and tapped the glasses until the thermal view appeared at the left. Before I could enlarge it, I noticed the red spot moving away from a blue one, and pushed myself back up. Korcz had jumped out from under the array and was running away from me across the field, unarmed. I tucked the left boa under my right forearm, closed my left eye, and fired two stoppers at him. After my hand came down from the second kick, I saw his collapsed body curling up on the ground, in the middle of a cloud of dust.

By the time I pulled the aero over to him and got out, he

had managed to drag himself to the edge of a gaping fissure that ran through the center of the stadium's field. He had also managed to pry loose a small knife that had been concealed under his arm. I took it from his almost-limp hand and threw it into the blackness of the crack, where it did not hit bottom, at least that I heard. As I went to turn him faceup, I saw the thick, bloody cross behind his right ear where one of the Xs had hit him. Based on the way he was struggling to move, I assumed the other one had hit him in the kidneys or lower spine. I turned him over, grabbed his lapels, and held his upper body over the edge of the crevasse.

"There are a lot of dead people down there," I said to him. "I'm sure they'd love some company." Korcz blinked his eyes at the blood that had seeped over to his face during his crawl. In my mind, I pictured this man walking up to D's car, my little girl staring at him from the back window. "Did. You. Kill. Darien. Anthony?"

"What?" he said, or something that resembled it, and blinked a few more times.

I pulled out the killer boa and held it to his face, my hand shaking from the rush of emotion, until I heard Twitch's voice say, "Is everything all right, sir?" And on the left side of my vision, because the editor had switched back to the falcon view, I saw myself from behind and above, the dark maw of the crack on the other side of me so big that it looked like it could swallow me whole, if I wasn't careful.

6

We took Korcz to the cathedral and locked him up, but within an hour it was obvious that this man was not the murderer. No fewer than five reliable and independent sources, both real and virtual, confirmed that he had flown into the Bay Area that morning, rather than three days ago, as Harris had said. He had come to visit his parents (the old couple), who still lived here. He was on vacation from a security job with an East Coast firm similar to ours, but smaller, and they had granted him his perfectly legitimate weapons clearance. He also had no explosives on him, or in the belongings we searched.

Why had he run, then? Seems that he had been guilty of some financial indiscretions years ago when he was an agent of BASS. Darien had handled the problem personally in a discreet and gracious manner, allowing him to leave without controversy, and even serving as a reference for him later on when he applied for his new job—which explained the periodic contact between the two men.

When Korcz heard that same morning that Darien had been killed, and then was confronted by a BASS posse, he thought that the clemency toward him had expired. The man also apparently had a deep-rooted paranoia about BASS leadership, which for some reason only Darien had been able to assuage. I made a mental note to ask him about this at some point before he was released, but now I was calling Harris from a net room in the castle, near the aero garage.

The tech beside me was busy with my special instructions when the tattooed freak appeared on the screen. I didn't want to endure his gloating, but there was a method to my madness.

"Sir Michael Ares," Harris barely managed to say in his talking-head voice, because he was laughing so hard. He clutched his stomach and rocked back and forth in his chair. *"Leads an assault on an innocent man, almost killing his geriatric, heart-patient parents"* (more laughing) "who immediately go to the press, *when they wake up*, describing the entire fiasco in vivid detail! This is Nirvana! The third heaven. Brainsmash, Headflip without the hangovers. A night with Marilyn—Monroe *and* Manson! I think it's on the news right now. . . ." He started fumbling with some of the screens beside him.

"I don't want to see it," I said. "You told me Korcz had been in town for three days, and that he had explosives on him."

"Beautiful, ain't it?" he said, proud of himself. "After you asked me about those names, our Tricky Dickies ran a net scan, and found out he had flown in and bought three tickets for the

Stick. I was hoping it would waste your time, at least, but I didn't even *dream* (Dream Base Outer Space) of a John Woo firefight! And you *phosgenated* his *mum*" laughing again "best use of toxic chemicals since the Haiti massacre!"

"You realize people could have been killed or wounded," I said.

"Torque 'em! That would have been Even Better Than the Real Thing." He was singing again; it was definitely time for this discussion to end.

"Harris," I said, and the excuse for a man raised his eyebrow as high as it could go, cocked his head to the side, and showed me all his multicolored teeth.

"Yes, my Cardinal Squeeze?"

"You've worn out your welcome," I said, and clicked him off. I asked the tech if he had successfully skirted the squatters' jam and recorded the conversation. He said yes, and did I want to see it? I said no, but copied it to my glasses, and headed for the garage.

As I headed north to the Ranch to visit Paul, the olive green and black of the castle and the early-evening sun receding behind me, I put the glasses on and brought up the reports and inquiries that had reached my desk during the day. One was merely an informational item, about a BASS aero that had been fired upon by a punk in Japantown who had built his own bazooka. Another was an "external employment transfer"—read *termination*—that I immediately signed with my code, trusting the evaluator who had submitted it. Beyond that, there was nothing significant or pressing, so I spent the rest of the trip learning about the plan to expunge the squatters, which had been intricately outlined two years ago, then shelved. I liked the plan, so I notified the necessary people that they should be prepared by tomorrow to implement it at a moment's notice.

When I had finished that project and was approaching Paul's Marin County residence, I finally began wondering why my boss and friend had seemed so troubled when he called me. He seemed to have no interest or excitement about the arrest of a possible suspect. Had he known that Korcz wasn't the man? Or was this unrelated? I only knew it was something of weight, because the only other times I had been invited to the Ranch were for social occasions involving our whole family.

As the memory of those family moments flooded into my mind, I pushed out the ones of the member I had lost and focused on the one who remained. I called Lynn, not really wanting to talk to her but thinking that I should. In fact, I used the audio on my glasses instead of the car phone, because I didn't want to have to look her in the eye. The answering message came on, and I started talking to our net system, half hoping that she wouldn't hear and answer.

"Hi, Lynn," I said. "I wanted to see how you're doing. Dumb question, I guess. And, uh, just wanted to let you know that I plan to sleep at home tonight, or at least try to sleep—"

"I don't know," she said, picking up the call. "I don't know."

"You don't know what?" I said, bracing myself.

"I don't know if I want you to come home."

We were both silent for a while. On my end, I was weighing whether this was a good or a bad turn of events.

"I'm just really confused," she finally continued. "Part of me wants to hurt you, hate you, for this. But part of me needs you. I'm not sure which part to listen to."

"I knew you would blame me for this," I said defensively, but feeling deep inside that I couldn't win this argument.

"Who else should I blame?" she answered, as if she had been rehearsing this in her mind. Then she said my answer before I could get it out. "The killer? Michael, sometimes it takes more than one person to make a murder. *I gave you the choice.* I let you decide about your job—probably because of some antiquated notion of male leadership that I got from the old lady . . ." Her straining voice was suddenly choked off by a series of sobs. "This is what I was afraid of!" Then more sobs.

I sat silently for a few moments, listening to the humming of the aero's engine. I thought about striking back or hanging up, but something told me that would mean more than I was ready for it to mean. I was truly beginning to think this might be the end for us, and for some reason the biggest part of me didn't want that.

"Lynn," I started, having no idea what I was going to say.

"No, Michael, listen," she interrupted in a softer voice. "I don't know what to think right now, so you need to do the thinking for us." She let out a combination of a sob and a chuckle. "Huh, that's from, uh—"

"Casablanca," I said.

"Yeah." It sounded like she was wiping her eyes and nose. "You just tell me if you want to come back here or not, that way I don't have to make the decision. Yeah. I guess I kinda want you to come home right now, I guess. But stay away if you want. You just tell me, so I know how it's gonna be."

"Well, I can't come right now—" I started.

"Fine. Goodbye," she blurted.

"No, wait!" I said, then paused to make sure she was still on the line. "I want to come home and be with you. But I'm here at Paul's right now. I have to meet with him for a few minutes, then I'll be there."

"Okay," she said. "But you have to be here. You remember all those times when you told me that and didn't make it? Well, this can't be one of them. I'm close, Michael, I'm on the edge. Don't let me fall off."

"I'll be there," I said. "Give me an hour at the most."

"I'll see you then," she said.

"I'll see you then," I echoed, and then tapped the glasses' audio off.

"I love you . . . ?" I said to nobody, after a few moments of silence.

By this time, the aero had automatically stopped and was undergoing a series of security scans at the perimeter of Paul's property. Marin had proven too broad an area to secure corporately like the Napa Valley, so the individual estates had developed their own fortresslike defenses. And Paul's was the best guarded, not only because he had access to the highest of high-tech resources through BASS but because his property was the most valuable.

Even beyond the obvious worth of three thousand acres secluded from any real neighbors, and the fifty million dollars' worth of architecture, the Ranch was a bona fide cultural and historical landmark. The land and the original buildings had been owned and built by a man named Lucas, who had produced about ten of the most well-known (and worshipped) flatmovies of all time. He had died just prior to the onset of holos, but versions of the virtual universe he created in his antiquated medium endured even until today, in various forms of entertainment.

As I hovered above the arid woodlands, waiting for the scans to conclude, I saw the inconspicuous gate on the ground in front of me and to my right. Someone with only a ground vehicle wouldn't have known the impressive estate was here unless they had been directed to it, and I was sure there was no sign at the road saying SKYWALKER RANCH (the original name, from one of the man's characters). But from the sky, I saw the congregation of Victorian-style buildings not too far north of the gate, and it was toward them that I directed the aero, once the clearance had been granted.

I watched and numbered the buildings in my mind as they grew closer: the inn for guests, the old firehouse, the stables, the theater, and the main house, along with accoutrements such as a vineyard and a baseball diamond. I also saw Paul's biggest addition to the original structures: an Olympic-size swimming pool that appeared to be open to the weather but actually was enclosed by an invisible transteel canopy, which somehow kept harmful rays from Paul and his family but still allowed them to enjoy the sun. It also kept the water and air under it warm in the winter. I remembered how Paul had introduced me to this marvel by lobbing toward the pool one of his son's balls, which bounced against nothing in the middle of the air and rolled slowly down more nothing until it was back on the ground. I remembered how Lynette had loved that trick, too, and my eyes watered up again.

I set the car down next to Paul's, and saw him stepping out of the main house to greet me, followed by his twin daughters, who had often played with Lynette, though they were a few years older. As I exited the car and walked to them, they each hung on one of their father's arms, and said, "Hi, Uncle Michael," almost simultaneously. Neither Paul nor I had brothers, so Lynette had addressed him in the same way, as "Uncle Paul."

"Hi, Hilly. Hi, Jessa," I replied. "How are you?" They said, "Fine," dutifully but sweetly, and then their father told them to get back to school, which I knew was actually inside the residence, staffed by live and virtual tutors. They did as he said, half skipping back into the house.

"They wanted to say hi," Paul said, the same pained look on his face, then he started moving away. "Why don't we go over to the theater." I walked with him, asking where John was. "He's riding with Liria. The girls are behind in school, but he's ahead right now. They hate that." He forced a smile, and I scanned the horizon, as if I might see the horses carrying the young man in his teens and the Asian woman, whose stunning beauty was blemished only by the half-hidden sadness that always seemed to cling to her. Lynn and I had many times pondered its cause, concluding that it probably had something to do with a husband who, like me, was "out saving the world" and seldom at home.

"It *is* a nice night for a ride," I said as we reached the big building, realizing then that the pall that infected my friend had spread to me. A lump was tightening in my stomach as we opened the inner door and were immediately accosted by a wall of sound. Paul frowned and informed me, over the din, that John had left the player on. He stepped inside the theater toward the controls at its center, and I followed, taking in the awesome virtual scene all around me.

The holo flashed from one environment to another, in perfect cadence with the rhythm of the music, sometimes displaying various settings in different places at the same time. I soon realized that this particular holo was depicting a medley of moments from the life of the singer, who was alternately shown bellowing his lyrics passionately. Amid the barrage of utterly realistic images from his childhood and adolescence (Christmas gifts, a funeral, his first sexual encounter, his father yelling, etc.), the man repeatedly disappeared and reappeared on another side of me. So did the other musicians, but the one stationary feature low on the horizon of the holo was the title of the song and the name of the artist: "Remembering" by Prisoner. I had heard it before.

Fading voices calling, flashing visions passing
A spiral of time, unhindered by
Remembering
Long lost joys emerging, conquered pains returning
A bittersweet thrill, forgetting but still
Remembering

Paul reached the controls, turned it off, and motioned to the plush seat I had bumped into while taking in the show. I sat down, and he did the same in another chair, planting his elbows on his knees and his head in his hands.

"I'm supposed to be the one feeling bad," I said to him, and he grunted, rubbing his eyes. "What's wrong?"

He shifted in his seat with his head down for a few minutes. Apparently, he was still working on whether or not he should tell me.

"You remember that I told you I was going to talk with the old man," he finally said. I nodded. "Well, I've had some suspicions since . . . last night really. So I tested them today when I was talking to him about you and D. . . ." He rubbed his eyes some more, looking simultaneously angry, despondent, and desperate. "And *I can't believe it* . . . but they've proven to be true."

"Paul," I said sympathetically, leaning forward. "Tell me what it is."

After a moment, he seemed to gather enough moral courage, and looked up at me.

"I know who killed your daughter," he said.

I jerked back, upright again, staring into his anguished eyes.

"Who?" I asked, barely a whisper.

He put his face back down in his hands, and said, "You did."

7

My initial response to Paul's revelation had two very odd qualities. The first was that I immediately found myself looking around the large room, which I suppose was the result of a subconscious prompting to make sure I was really there, or that no one was watching. The high walls and ceiling were designed to hide the holo equipment in them, and the wide, flat floor was filled with rows of deluxe chairs like the one I was sitting in, capable of tilting and rotating in any direction desired by its occupant.

The other peculiarity of my nascent reaction to Paul's words was that I somehow had a feeling, in defiance of all plausibility, that they were true. This feeling was short-lived, though, because just moments later I began to wonder how they possibly could be. Paul obviously wasn't joking, however—I saw that in his eyes. And I had never seen him exhibit any signs of encroaching insanity. So I just looked at him, numbly waiting for him to explain.

"Let me start—" he said, then hesitated, digging down deep for courage again. "Let me start from the beginning." He hesitated again. "Look, Michael. I'll be honest with you. I don't know if I should be telling you this—that's why you had to come out here, away from the walls with ears. But you're my friend, and he's gone way too far this time." I wondered who "he" was, but just continued watching him as he talked with his head down, trying to convince himself. "Some things are just . . . *over the line.* I've seen too many of them, and I can't look the other way anymore." He pulled a handkerchief out and wiped the sweat off his brow.

"Years ago, *my father*," he said those words with tight lips, "launched a black op called Mind Lift, meaning stealing your mind or maybe improving it, or both, I don't know. The initial research and development was being done in the second lab at the cathedral—the one that's underground. The original idea was to send criminals back out into the streets, so that we could observe through them, and even use them for arrests when the time came. But soon the old man started talking about doing it to peacers. I wasn't for it, of course, so it was pulled from that lab. But I *knew* it had been transplanted somewhere else, because there was no way he was gonna just give up that kind of brainpower, not to mention all the time and money that'd already gone into it."

"Paul," I interrupted. "I'm not following you."

"What part?"

"What were they developing?"

"Implants, chips. For wireless neural interface." He pointed to the back of his head. "Jackless two-way communication with the carrier's brain. One way, to see and hear through him; the other way, to control him." He was now pointing at the front of his head and away from it, alternately.

"Control him?"

He nodded. "You've heard of this, right?"

"I know that there were rumors of it in other countries," I recalled. "And they had a meeting in Geneva to deal with it."

"Right, right," Paul said. "And it was about that time that the old man pulled it from the lab. But he moved it. He told me where back then, and even gave me limited access, but I didn't want to press him about it. My mother was sick and he was already starting to get a little crazy, cloistered up there in his dark domain. But I always wondered if he and his need-to-know goons went on with the peacer plans."

"So did they?" I asked, the lump in my stomach becoming even more noticeable.

"Yes!" His head in his hands again. "Oh God, Michael, they did! And *I am so sorry* that I didn't find out until now. Some friend I've turned out to be . . ." His shoulders shook from the sobs trying to escape. A light finally went on in my mind, and the knot behind my belt turned into a stabbing pain.

"You're saying I have one of those things in my head?" I forced out, then tried to breathe. Paul looked up at me again.

"This morning, when we found out the murderer could have been someone D and your daughter both knew," he looked down again, "and it could have been someone from BASS, I got the wild idea in my head. So when I told the old man about it, I asked him point-blank if Mind Lift had really died. He was more than evasive, man—he just stopped talking to me. I know him, Michael. That was when I knew." He saw me shaking my head in disbelief, staring at a seat beside him, and continued.

"He's lost it, man. Ever since my mother died, it's gotten worse and worse. He has this sadistic streak, and the power has done something to him. Nobody sees him like I do, believe me, but I don't even know him anymore. For some reason he saw D as a threat; I think maybe because D found out something about the project. He was asking me some questions related to it in the last few weeks—and now he's dead."

"You're saying," I gasped, my head still moving back and forth, "that your father . . . *used me* . . . to kill D? He made me do this, with some wetware in my head?" Like most people who were successful or hoped to be successful, I had vowed long ago to stay free of any such implants, because it was assumed to be a safer route to avoiding potential risks to health and privacy. And now it seemed that all the suspicions and fears were being proven true.

"Forgive me, Michael, please."

"This isn't about *you*, Paul," I snapped, then tried to change my tone when I saw how it stung him. "I have questions. You've got to help me with this."

"Absolutely. We're in this together," he said, then asked me if I wanted a drink. "This's got to be a hell of a nightmare—I can't even imagine." I declined the drink, then asked my first question.

"How did this thing get in my head?"

"Early on, after you came," Paul answered. "I don't know a lot of the details, but they put you out somehow, then erased the memory of it."

"That's possible?" I asked.

"Oh yeah. You've got to realize, Michael: between what's on the hill and what we have in the Silicon Valley, BASS owns *the most* cutting-edge technology in the world. World leaders aren't kissing the old man's ass just for aerocar science, they're into this neuro stuff, too. Min isn't just a bodyguard, he's a showpiece, a floor model of a *personal* computer, with a capital *P.* He's got those two custom jackpatches behind his ear, which you can see, but he can also send and receive wireless from *inside.* What you see in your glasses, he sees without them. Neuro-optical retinal implants."

"So if I have this in me, why can't they hear what we're saying right now?"

"Right, good question," he said, progressing out of the self-pity mode and into one of industry. "After I talked to the old man, I knew you were busy at the Stick, so I paid a visit to the black-op lab in the valley. Like I said, I have access—but even I had to endure four checkpoints and a fake floor before I could get there. And even then, the technocreep I talked to could only tell me certain things, and show me certain things. The old man has a lot going on that even his son doesn't know, believe me."

"What did you find at the lab?" I said, hurrying him on.

"I went under the pretense of investigating D's murder, because I knew they wouldn't tell me anything about you, or anyone else who has the chip. Hell, the guy I talked to probably didn't know himself who did it, they have so many layers of intrigue. But I asked him if they monitored the chips, and he said no, they only activate them, especially the older ones, when there's a particular job to be done or a specific memory to be accessed, erased, or whatever. He explained this, something about cost-effectiveness and the danger of seepage in the brain; I didn't understand much of it.

"But then he dropped a bomb on me: he told me that D's chip—yes, he had one, too—had been recovered by the scene techs last night and sent to him this morning. It was almost totally destroyed by the blast, but a recovery process yielded some data, including—" He reached behind him to the place on his belt where I wear my guns, as I instinctively tensed, and brought out a small datafold. He slid a tiny disk out, gripped it between finger and thumb, and waved it in front of me. "A picture of the murderer," he finished.

When he got no reaction from me except a deer-in-the-headlights stare, he reached over to the entertainment console and inserted the disk into a special plug-in attachment, which was necessary because this kind of storage device was used only by poor people who had no wireless tech. Within seconds, one wall of the theater, like an old flatmovie screen, displayed the image. It was a slightly blurry but recognizable shot of a black figure silhouetted against a backdrop of various shades of intense light. An uninformed observer would probably never have been able to identify the perpetrator by looking at the image, but to those who knew what they were looking at, like Paul and me, there could be no doubt.

The last person Darien Anthony saw was Michael Ares.

I closed my eyes and involuntarily visualized the scene from what must have been D's perspective. The dark shape now imprinted in my mind moved closer, revealing my own features as they contacted the dim light from inside the car. I looked to the right and saw Lynette pressed up against the window, saying "Daddy! Daddy! . . ."

"This is the kind of evidence you were hoping for," Paul said, gesturing to the screen and mercifully rescuing my mind from its trip to hell. "But what can you do with it? The old man may be twisted, but he's also a genius. When the investigating officer *is* the murderer, he would never suspect himself, so the crime will never be solved. If he *does* find any evidence that points to himself, he would ignore or suppress it. And you never would've even had any idea, if I hadn't poked around and been inclined to tell you." He grunted and shook his head. "If I wasn't thinking of a way right now to put him out of his misery, I would admire the old bastard."

"How could I have killed them when I was at the symphony with Lynn?" I asked.

"What did you do before that?" Paul asked. "Do you remember?"

"I gave Lynette to D at the castle," I said, straining my traumatized brain. *Fading voices calling, flashing visions passing.* "Then I went to pick up Lynn at her friend's."

"Was there enough time in there that you could have stopped at D's?"

"I don't know," I said. *A spiral of time* . . . "I'm not sure exactly when I did what. I just know I got Lynn around seven, because that's when I was supposed to pick her up."

"Hmph." He nodded. "Tech put the time of the murder between six and eight. By the way, had you planned ahead of time to see the Requiem, or did you decide on the spur of the moment?"

"It was after I got Lynn."

"Hmph," he said again, and I caught his drift. Mozart's Requiem is, of course, a Mass for the dead. *Hostias! Sanctus!* I looked up again at the silhouette on the screen, holding my eyes open this time to keep the image stationary.

"How can I get the imp out of my head?" I asked.

"You can't," Paul answered. "In case anyone ever found out, they made it impossible to remove without the death of the carrier. The old man probably figured he could use it as leverage if any of you discovered the truth. He probably can kill you with it if he wants—that's why we need to sit on it right now and plan how to deal with him. You can't do anything reckless or impulsive, Michael. You understand that, right?"

I had drifted off, wondering why Saul had not just killed Darien with the chip, but then I realized that he would have been taking a chance that someone might discover it as the cause of death and trace it. Better to have a trusting, oblivious pawn blow him to bits, along with my beautiful little girl . . .

"What was that again?" I asked.

"You have to act like everything is normal right now, until we can come up with a plan," Paul repeated. "He has to pay for this, no question—but any rash moves will cost us our lives as well."

"I understand," I said. "What do you have in mind?" I wanted to kill the old man, of course, though I knew being caught would bring a death sentence. But would his only son want that, too?

"I don't know yet," he answered. "We can't even get *near* him as long as Min is around. In addition to his other upgrades, the giant also has state-of-the-art global combat augmentations."

Though no one had told me this before, I had wondered about it ever since the time I saw the huge creature move into a defensive position in front of Saul, from a few feet behind, when we had encountered a perceived threat. Actually, I hadn't seen Min move at all—he was that fast.

"I would have to find out when he's going in for maintenance," Paul finished, and noticed my puzzled look.

"You can't take something like him down to your local glasses shop," he explained. "He has to go right back to Chinatown Underground, where he was put together." As he said this, I pictured that remarkable part of the city where the local Chinese money (and a lot from elsewhere) had rebuilt the flattened Chinatown, covering the surface with replicas of the former buildings to preserve their "cultural heritage," but also adding below them a shiny new mall-like town, which stretched twenty levels down and almost a mile in width. Paul explained that one of the Underground's primary industries was cyberware, and the techs there, along with their counterparts in eastern Asia, had cornered the market on legal, autonomous, high-level implants like the ones Min was sporting.

I remembered hearing that Japan had once been the leading technological nation in Asia, and the most likely to win the race to such innovations. But after the acquisition of Hong Kong and the overdue rise of a full-blown technological revolution on the mainland, China soon left her smaller neighbors in the dust. About ten years ago, they became the primary pioneers of global cybernetics, partly because most other "civilized" nations had not been shameless enough to dive so eagerly and openly into the process of making men into machine-men, or cyborgs, as they have always been called.

"I'll take that drink now," I told Paul, who stood up and headed for the bar, which was annexed to the side of the theater. Unfortunately, he left my silhouette on the screen. I stared at it, letting each shade of light on the outside, and the darkness within, etch itself into my eyes, mind, and soul. As Paul returned with the drink in his hand, I popped the little disk out of his player.

"Are there any other copies of this?" I asked.

"No," Paul answered. "I deleted the source copy and put it on that old disk because it has no wireless capacity. So no one can extract or copy the image unless they physically plug it into their hardware. But if you want to get rid of the evidence on the disk, I would destroy it utterly or lose it where it can't be found.

Just deleting it would leave some kind of digital residue that an accomplished tech might be able to retrieve."

"Thanks," I said, and stuck the little circle in my datafold.

"I hope this helps," Paul said, handing me the drink.

"I just killed three people, including my own daughter," I said, downing the whole glass with a grimace. "But I don't know which feels worse—that or the thought of facing her mother."

8

I've never been much of a drinker, but when I have imbibed, it has almost always made me feel happier. By the time the autopilot informed me that we had reached the Napa Valley, however, I was downright angry. The intense emotion seemed beyond the reach of logic as I glared at the food truck parked at the base of my house, resenting it for intruding on my privacy, even though I knew it came every week and the driver was perfectly innocent, cleared by every security check imaginable.

As my aero descended out of the darkening sky and landed next to the truck, I tried to contain a desire to load incendiary rounds into one of my boas and abuse the other vehicle. What I thought of doing to the driver, who was coming out of the house, was even uglier. He said hello, and I managed to grunt and swerve around him, heading in through the front door.

Lynn was in the kitchen, putting away the food. She kept doing it even after she noticed me, and didn't say anything.

"I'm here," I said, from just inside the doorway, testing the waters. "Like I said."

"Thanks, I think," she said, not altogether scornfully. "What did you find out?" I hesitated, not expecting this so soon. She stopped what she was doing and looked at me.

"Nothing," I said, too abruptly. "Nothing at all, unfortunately. We do have, uh, we *did* have a suspect, but it was a wash." We looked at each other too long, but then she turned and continued her chore. "What have you been doing?" I ventured, stepping closer.

"Nothing, too," she said, and then turned back to face me, a bag of frozen peas in her hand, when she sensed me approaching. I wondered what it would feel like to be hit in the face with the peas, but as it turned out, I faced no such threat, at least so far. Instead, she started crying.

"I was watching you and me in old holos, before she was born." She wiped her face with her free hand. "I thought I should try to be glad for what I still have." I started to step closer to her, to hold her, but then she gestured to my right. "And I was reading that book."

I looked over, and on the kitchen's center counter was an old book called *Black Death*, with a picture of rats on the cover. The price tag, for some meager amount, was still on it.

"I got it at a thrift store a long time ago," she said. "And finally pulled it out today. It's funny . . . when I got it, I thought,

I'll buy this and keep it for when I'm really down, so I can remember that I'm not so bad off." She laughed, a half sob. "It actually works." It did seem that the thought of it had calmed her presently. And I couldn't overestimate the therapeutic effect of a book that she had found at a thrift store . . . those were two of her best friends, books and thrift stores, even though she could read the same thing on the net and had enough money to buy things new (a hundred times over).

"What's it about?" I asked. The moment for hugging her seemed to have passed. I reached for the peas and helped her put the rest of the food away as she explained.

"It's about the 1300s, when like half of the known world was wiped out by a plague. In less than four years. They left bodies in houses and streets to rot because no one wanted to get near 'em. Whole towns and cities were abandoned, people leaving all their stuff and sleeping out on the ground to get away from everyone else. Back then, it was a miracle if *anyone* in your family didn't die."

"I see what you mean," I said, but still felt the anger boiling within me, though it seemed restrained to some degree by my affection for Lynn. It didn't seem an effect of alcohol at all—but it did remind me of the effects of some drugs I had taken a long time ago when I was in the military. "Let's go sit down," I added after finishing the food and closing the cooler.

As we walked into the next room and found a couch, I was thinking we might actually get through this night. Her melancholy but moderate manner might have been an ongoing effect of the "medication" the old man had given her, but I wasn't about to complain. Now, if only I could keep myself from exploding . . .

"I'm sorry, Michael," she said, leaning on my shoulder and putting her hand on my chest. She started rubbing it gently, and I started to think that maybe this whole thing would actually end up bringing us closer, instead of tearing us apart. But then Lynn went on. "I was wrong at first. I held you responsible, too much, for what happened. My mind was screaming, 'He killed her! He murdered our daughter!' It was weird. But I know it's wrong. You didn't kill our sweetheart. Somebody out there did. And God, maybe. I don't know . . ."

Then she noticed that my muscles had tensed—an involuntary response to her words. She stopped touching me, and sat up straight.

"What's wrong?"

I didn't answer right away, but when I did, I said, "Nothing."

"Does that make you mad, that I had those thoughts?" Lynn said.

"Yeah," I answered, through tight lips. "Maybe that's it."

"Well, that's just great," she said, scratching her head violently. "I wait all day to tell you this, thinking we can . . . *commiserate* together, and you get mad at me." She stood up and raised her voice more. "I got four calls from funeral services today—those *vultures*—something that *you* should be taking care of anyway. Can't you change the filter so that kinda junk can't get through, like I've *asked you to do* infinity-plus-twenty times?"

Infinity-plus-twenty profane expressions were bouncing around in my brain—but I had learned the hard way that using any of them with Lynn created major walls that didn't come down for weeks, at least. Instead, I forced myself to say, "Sit down and bear with me, please." She did, but on the other end of the couch. "We'll win the Nobel Peace Prize, if we can somehow stay together through this."

"Is 'this' more than Lynnie?" she asked. "I feel like you're hiding something from me." I would have laughed at this uncanny sixth sense of hers, if only it were being used on someone other than me. She crossed her arms and scrutinized me silently.

"Look, Lynn," I finally said, "I'm not doing well right now. I had a drink at Paul's, and it's done something to me. Or it's the stress. Or both. Can't we just drop the paranoia, and commiserate, like you said?"

I looked down, praying that she wouldn't say, "You didn't answer my question." But she did.

"I don't even remember the question!" I fired in her direction, twisting to face her. "I'm trying to tell you, *I'm not doing too well.* Maybe your pharmaceutical wonder and your cathartic book have helped you to get over this, but I'm not there, okay!"

"I am *hardly* 'over this,' and I can't believe you would say that." She let out a gasp of disgust to match the look on her face, and got up again. This time, she pointed at the front door.

"Go back out and find the monster who killed my daughter!" she said, still pointing. "It's the only thing I need you for anymore." She spun and stomped up the stairs, out of sight. After watching the empty stairs for a few moments, I turned straight and stared ahead at nothing.

Don't have to look any further for the monster, I thought. *He's sitting on your couch.*

I continued to sit utterly motionless for a while, feeling several varieties of pain grow in every part of me. I thought about opening the book on the Black Death, but it was too far away from me, and I couldn't get up. *That's what this is,* I thought, *the Black Death.* It was settling all around me, seeping into my pores, threatening to drive out all health—physical, mental, and emotional. I pressed my eyes closed, clenched my teeth, and said the word *no* through them with every outward breath for about a minute. But when the muscles in my arms and gut began to cramp from tensing for so long, I realized I couldn't go on like this. *I need to tell Lynn,* I thought. *It's only right, and someone has to help me carry this . . .*

I opened my eyes to see if she might have come back, and when I saw that she had not, I began moving my head around slowly, studying the room. I took in the two Monet prints on the walls and then stared at the real one for a while, the trains in *The Gare Saint-Lazare* forever readying but never actually leaving the station.

It was while my eyes were locked on the ornate mantel above the fireplace that my conscious mind caught up with my subconscious, and I realized why I was looking around at my house: *Saul didn't want me to see it while it was being built!* I had mentioned to him one time, during the construction of the house, that I was planning on driving up here to see the workers' progress. But he had dissuaded me. . . .

"Don't do that, 007," he had said, "Let them surprise you with the finished product."

"But Lynn and I gave you those requests for the design," I said. "It would be interesting for us to see how they're being implemented."

"I'm sure," the old man had replied, but then lowered his head and glared authoritatively at me from the top of his eyes. "But don't do that, Michael."

I remember being puzzled at his insistence, but I wrote it off as another eccentricity, and forgot about it. But now it took on a new significance. He had built me this house, and had done so in secrecy, for a purpose. There had to be some reason that he hadn't wanted me to see what the builders were doing, and I couldn't think of a better one than *surveillance*. They must have rigged the house so that Saul could keep an eye on me. And if that was the case, I couldn't tell Lynn anything here without running the risk of being observed. After a few moments of anger at the thought, it actually made me feel better—because now I had another excuse to keep the truth from her.

This mild sense of relief was enough to allow my exhausted frame to drift into sleep, which turned out to be quite fitful. Nightmares followed one another in rapid succession. . . .

The choir at the Requiem bellowed something in Latin that I didn't understand, but I acted like I did. As my eyes scanned their faces, I saw that one of them was Lynn and the next was

Lynette. Her mother seemed to be spitting out the lyrics, but my little girl was angelic as ever, wearing the ponytails I loved so much.

Then Harris was reading the Latin words from an old vinyl record on one of his infomercials, in his "talking head" voice. He muttered something that I couldn't make out, but I knew it was something that he had said to me at some point. And I knew it was important. But the scene shifted before I could ask him.

Then, sometime later, floating in the middle of a dark sea, bobbing back and forth like a small boat, was D's driveway. I stepped inside it as the gate opened, holding something metal between the fingers and palm of my right hand, and approached the car. D recognized me, and started opening the window, and the little girl in the backseat was up at her window, saying something to me through the glass. But I didn't really know them. I squeezed the trigger on the disk in my hand, bowled it under the car, and jumped back, seeing a burst of white light through my eyelids. I felt hot all over, and opened my eyes to see that I was scorched from the blast.

From the flames of the wreckage stepped Saul Rabin, leaning on his cane and laughing maniacally. With the fire behind him, he appeared as a silhouette, all dark except for his eyes, which glowed bright red like the flames. The light from his eyes reached out toward me, pressing like fingers into my head, until the razor-sharp piece of metal inside my brain started moving around, churning and slashing through my gray matter like a farmer's sickle.

• • •

The pain became so intense that it woke me up. I was still upright on the couch, but I was now sweating and my head was throbbing with the echoes of the nightmare wound. I glanced at the clock on the wall, noting that the two hours I had just slept were two more than the night before. That explained the intensity of my dreams—but what about their content? Driven by a morbid fascination, and something nagging at the back of my mind, I reviewed them as best I could.

The one I remembered most was the last, of course. Were the images of the murder from my *memory*, as they seemed to be, or a reconstruction from the facts I knew? Certainly the old man hadn't stepped out of the fire, but the rest of it was real enough that I never wanted to endure it again. And what about Harris? Hadn't he said something significant to me? In vain I tried to recall it from my two discussions with him, but then I remembered the glasses, and put them on.

I called up the audio recording of my first talk with him, and listened from the beginning. Halfway into it, I suddenly remembered the prerecorded message that had gotten through to me earlier, and found that. In a few moments, I had what I was looking for.

"Prayer is what you'll need, Mick, when he stops liking you Just the Way You Are [singing again] and morphs your ass into goo. Or maybe he'll do a mind lift, a head hijack, a brain boost, a personality pinch . . . jerk with your neuros and make you into someone he likes."

I rewound a little, and heard again, "*jerk with your neuros.*" And he had even used the phrase *mind lift.* Did Harris know about this? If so, it was a pretty high-level leak. Or had he been involved with it before he left BASS? While the glasses were on, I made a note to check into this, and came across the reminder to talk to Korcz about his paranoia regarding our upper-level leadership. This cued me to search the Web for some more information, and I thought of using the room system like I usually did, but then realized that my glasses were more likely to be private. Most homes with net rooms had only one or two at the most, because that was all normal people could afford, but in ours almost every room was equipped with the technology, and it occurred to me that Saul might have been using that equipment to keep an eye on me. I imagined there was some risk in going on the net in any way for what I wanted, but I decided to limit it to a few minutes and hope it didn't come back to bite me.

So, staying in the glasses, I entered a search for "neural manipulation." It took a while to get it started because I had to key the words in letter by letter, using the glasses' mouse, because I didn't want to say them out loud. Numerous links came up, and the large majority of them confirmed what Paul had claimed—that there was a broad consensus among experts in related fields that it could be done. There seemed to be no documented cases of its actually happening, but that might have been because the Geneva Accords put a serious cramp in research by forbidding any legal development. The political and corporate leaders who met there certainly were worried about the possibility, and there were many other Web sites filled with paranoia about it.

I modified the search to "Saul Rabin neural manipulation," and nothing came up that was directly related. There were many entries about Saul Rabin and manipulation, but they were all critiques of his governing decisions and leadership style. Many of these sites referenced his famous last press conference many years ago, after which he had decided to stay away from the media and let Paul and D act as the public spokesmen for BASS. I had seen the video of it many times before but wanted to watch it again with "new eyes," so I brought up one of the clips listed.

"Please comment on the repression of minorities in San Francisco," a female reporter says.

"Who's being repressed?" Saul answers.

"LGBT and PPB groups, for one."

"Nonsense," Saul says in an angry tone. "There are no new laws under BASS that didn't exist before it. We haven't even made any public statements about any of those lifestyle preferences . . . no new laws or even statements concerning gays, not for lesbians, not for bisexuals, not for transgenders, not for pedophiles, not for polyamorists, and not for bestialists, or for any other types of people for that matter. And don't forget that BASS has given staggering amounts of money to AIDS and AIMS research and treatment."

"Then why have so many people left the city since you've come to power?"

"A lot of criminals have left the city," the Mayor says, turning to his son next to him and flashing that twisted smile obstructed by his scar.

"But what about many activists who have no criminal records?"

"I don't know, ask them," he says, getting irritated again. "Nobody makes anybody stay or go."

"We *have* asked them, and they say that you want to control people too much."

"No, they want too much control!" Pointing at the reporter. "I am the duly elected leader of this city. We can't have too many hands on the wheel; we won't get anywhere."

"You were elected *after* you were in power and many people had left, fearing what you would do. . . ."

"I can't help how people read me, or if they read me wrong. And at the beginning, we *really* couldn't have too many hands on the wheel . . . when you're crashing, that's the last thing you need."

"You are a tyrant, like every other one in history," she says with a loud voice, more to the crowd than to Saul. "Who can only rule by control and manipulation!"

"Listen, you little bitch," the old man is shouting now, "I'd control things *more* if I could, and if I knew it was best for the people of this city . . . and I'd manipulate your punk ass right out of it!"

At this point Paul stepped in, calmed down his father, and concluded the press conference in a softer and gentler way; and, along with D, had conducted all of them ever since. I remembered hearing that afterward, Saul was regretful about this ugly scene, which was broadcast all over the world, of course. I also realized that it was probably a key event (or setback) in his wife's efforts to reform his speech patterns, and I wondered if she had chastened him for his comments about control as well. But since Mrs. Rabin had died seven years ago, I could see how he might now have reverted to the control problem, even though he continued to honor her memory in the language department.

Not wanting to risk any more exposure on the Web, I took off the glasses. I was locked in a living hell without a key, but at least things were becoming more clear in my mind. I used to view Saul Rabin's last press conference as impressive evidence of his chutzpah, that he was not willing to back down to special-interest groups pushing their agendas. But now I was starting to see it as oppressive, rather than impressive.

I heard movement from the stairs, and a guilty feeling shot through me. I sat up straight and wiped the sweat on my face with my sleeve, looking over just in time to see Lynn appear from the stairs. She looked briefly at me, went across the kitchen to get her Black Death book, and walked back to the stairs. As she started up them, she said, "I love you," without looking at me, then disappeared.

I shook my head, thinking that loving her was a lot easier than understanding her.

I forced myself to my feet, still groggy, thankful that some of my anger had been swallowed by the sleep, or maybe released by the dreams. I traversed the kitchen and climbed the stairs. Lynn was in our room, on the bed, reading the book with her knees drawn up in front of her. I assumed the same position next to her, reading along with her for a little while, hoping to find comfort in the book myself.

She was at a part where the author was describing flagellism, a religious practice that arose during the plague. It was an attempt on the part of some fanatics to appease the wrath of God and end the suffering by inflicting pain upon themselves. They thought this self-abuse could somehow atone for the sins that had caused the pestilence. The author quoted from a fourteenth-century eyewitness named Jean Froissart.

> The penitents went about, coming first out of Germany. They were men who did public penance and scourged themselves with whips of hard knotted leather with little iron spikes. Some made themselves bleed very badly between the shoulder blades and some foolish women had cloths ready to catch the blood and smear it on their eyes, saying it was miraculous blood. While they were doing penance, they sang very mournful songs about nativity and the passion of Our Lord. The object of this penance was to put a stop to the mortality, for in that time . . . at least a third of all the people in the world died . . .

I continued reading for a while, but didn't find that it made me feel any better. The poor wretches who went through the plague had it bad, for sure—but at least none of them had murdered their own daughter and friend. And it was beginning to bother me more and more that the subject of this cruel deity seemed to be popping up at every turn during my ordeal . . . I had enough to worry about with the enemies I could see. On the other hand, the book's references to death and atonement did lead me to some ideas about my situation that were strangely cathartic. Paul was right, of course, that acting on my own, I could never take out the old man without dying in the process. But perhaps that was exactly what I needed to do—take revenge on my enemy and make restitution for my own crimes in a glorious orgy of mortal violence. And I began to feel that the resulting oblivion would be far preferable to living with all this.

But the metaphysical shadow that had been following me prevented me from committing to that course. As I thought about how I would carry out this murder/suicide and pictured myself doing it, the theme of Hamlet's most famous speech nagged me. I had seen the play dozens of times, and years ago I had even memorized the "to be or not to be" soliloquy. I couldn't remember it word-for-word now, but I knew the point. What if there was a life after this one? And what if we have to answer for what we do here? That fear of the unknown is enough to keep even the bravest man from taking his own life, according to the Bard. I took comfort from this amid my own cowardice, because I had to admit that even if my death would make everything right, I still didn't want to die. . . .

At some time during my ruminations, an exhausted Lynn gave up on the book and rested her head on my shoulder. As I watched her fall asleep, I again felt a tiny surge of hope that we could somehow come out on the other end of this. So I decided to go with Paul's more cautious plan, hoping that I could manage to suppress my craving to blow the old man into a thousand bits, or dismember him slowly.

"Act like everything is normal," Paul had said. I would try

my best for now, but if my friend's approach took too long, I would take it as a sign that Saul Rabin and I should pay for our sins together, in one bloody act of expiation.

At dawn I left Lynn sleeping in the bed, showered, dressed, took off in the aero, and checked the glasses, just as I had the morning before. Once again there were two messages from Paul, and a clip of Harris, which Paul had attached.

"You need to see this," he said. "Harris fell into it somehow, and got it rated by Reality G. They say it's legit."

Reality Guaranteed was the premier "genuineness evaluation" service in the world, formed under federal American law years ago, during the initial rise of computer crime. In addition to identity theft and credit fraud, audiovisual technology had progressed so far by then that any Tom, Dick, or Harry could produce albums, movies, and various forms of pornography featuring popular media figures, without the stars themselves ever being involved. These were marketed so widely on the wild wild web that certification with services like Reality G became necessary for consumers to know whether their purchases were authentic. The news could be faked, too, so a video clip couldn't survive with any credibility unless it received their stamp of approval.

The end of Paul's message said that this particular clip had already been distributed and broadcast on numerous news services, but because it had started with Harris, he sent me the freak's "world premiere" showing.

". . . And it seems that the James Bond of BASS is looking

more like a Benedict Arnold," Harris was saying when the clip began, with the usual nausea-inducing, ADHD-directed visuals flashing and swirling around him. He began singing again: "*Ooooh, really makes me wonder* if he had something to do with the recent Death By Dissection of his immediate superior! Nooooo, that could never be, right? A war hero confined to an office job could never get itchy for more action or power, would he? Naaaaaah. Don't worry about this Dark Knight, folks—just hope to Hades that he doesn't want *your* job."

A little hand from one of his tattoos stretched out to make a huge one, which pointed at the viewer.

"And as for you, *Mikey Mouse*, when they put you away in that overgrown dungeon formerly known as a church, well, What More Can I Say? . . . *Don't bend over for the soap!*"

As he was laughing hysterically, the clip of me came on. It was a close-up from a room in the castle that I didn't recognize immediately, and this is what I was saying:

"I'm sick of this place. I'd like to burn it down. I'm sick of the old man, and I'd like to slit his throat and drink his blood."

It was me, no question. And I even remembered saying it.

9

On the way to the city, I made a few calls to various depart-ments regarding the murder investigation. The circulating video clip made me even more uneasy than I already was, because it made me look like a loose cannon, and I was afraid that someone might make a connection between me and D's death before Paul and I could confront the old man. I had experienced similar smears before, but none when I was actually guilty of a crime. So I tried to look busy about finding the killer. There were no leads yet, of course.

The disk with the incriminating image on it was burning a hole in my datafold, but so far I had thought of only one way to dispose of it safely, and that would have to wait, for now. I couldn't ask Harris about the black op at this time, because if he knew anything more about it, his comments might be overheard, and if he didn't know anything, I wouldn't feel as good about what I was planning to do to him.

By the time I reached the castle, I was fairly sure where and how the incriminating video clip of me had been taken. So I parked the aero, rode the elevators, and passed through two security checkpoints until I reached our executive lounge. Once there, I tried to recall where we had each been sitting during the conversation, and which camera would have captured me from the angle in the clip. When I was fairly sure it was the visible camera (a nickel-size protrusion high on one wall) rather than the hidden one, I headed for Internal Security.

Upon entering the ISec floor, I paused for a moment, then walked to Tara's office, feeling the usual mixture of pleasure and guilt, but with an extra dose of guilt this time. *She is the most appropriate contact for this,* I rationalized, and then felt more guilty for having to explain myself to myself. Before I could ring her door, she appeared behind me.

"Can I help you, Mr. Ares?" her voice said. I turned, and tried not to notice how good she looked. Instead of drinking in her milk-chocolate skin and dark brown hair, I tried to picture Lynn's pale white and streaked gold. Tara's handsome frame, almost as tall as mine, was harder to ignore, as were the memories that immediately flooded into my mind. I had managed to delete some through time and practice, but others were harder to erase. And seeing her reminded me of D, who had taken great pleasure in congratulating me for "expediting the process of evolution" by dating one of "his people." I had pointed out to him on several occasions that Tara's mother was almost white, to which he had shrugged and pronounced it a "transitional stage."

My rush of emotions must have shown through, at least slightly, because she cocked her head and looked at me curiously, but also hopefully. "I would really like to help you," she finished with a caring smile. For some reason, this sparked the odd feeling of anger that was hanging around inside me, which in this situation actually helped me to regain my composure and stay focused on the business at hand.

"Yes, you can, in fact," I said tersely. "I want you to find me something in the camera room." She concealed her feelings about as well as I had, saying, "Follow me, then," through a disappointed sigh.

A few moments later, we were seated in front of a bank of screens as the software searched through years of digital video to find the images we wanted. While she was setting up the search by fiddling with the hardware around us, she glanced over at me almost as much as she looked at the equipment, and she leaned across me a few times to reach some of it. She did that exactly two times, to be precise, and I did notice her nearness more than I wanted to admit. I tried to think of Lynn again, not wanting to add to my already overwhelming load of guilt.

The system must have found the keys it had been given, because a screen in front of us flashed on, showing a scene of three men reclining and talking in the executive lounge. It was shot from the camera I had seen, which was looking down on Paul, D, and me from its spot on the wall. I told Tara to rewind it, and we watched the whole discussion:

". . . But she didn't know," D said. "I'll check again in a few days."

"That reminds me," I offered. "I talked to Franken yesterday." I noticed that I was smoking one of those legal cigarettes, though as usual I didn't seem to be enjoying it very much. I had given up the real ones—finally—when I came aboard BASS's tight ship.

"What did he say?" Paul asked. I took a moment to respond, trying to remember the exact words.

" 'I'm sick of this place. I'd like to burn it down. I'm sick of the old man, and I'd like to slit his throat and drink his blood.' "

Paul and D looked at each other and snickered. "I'm not surprised," Paul said. "He's on about ten different drugs, the second five balancing the first five—you know how it goes. He can't be held responsible for his actions right now, but he also can't be an agent anymore."

"Let him go, and give him a class-C," Darien suggested, looking at Paul, who nodded.

I told Tara to pause it, and asked her how someone had gotten a close-up of me. "Like this," she answered as she zoomed in the view so that only my face was on the screen, the smoke floating in front of it. "Then they just copied it." It occurred to me that the smoke made me seem even more dangerous, because no one who saw the clip would know that the fake cancer stick was legal.

"So how many people could have done this?" I asked.

"You can count them on your hand—that I know. You saw how I needed your codes to access the upper levels." She reached forward and touched the tops of each of my fingers lightly, starting with the little one, as she named the suspects. "Rabin Senior, Rabin Junior, Anthony, and you." She touched the last finger a little longer, stretching out the word. Then she tapped my thumb. "Maybe the big bodyguard, I don't know. Because the old man has a personal security room upstairs in his suite, you know, with access to all the cameras. There's always at least a few of us here, so someone would have noticed if one of you big shots came in and was fiddling around with the database."

She thought for a few seconds, then nodded. "I would say the clip came from the penthouse terminal."

I knew that the only ones who had access to that equipment were the Rabins, so it was clear that the likeliest suspect was the old man. I also remembered that Harris had called me James Bond in his commentary on the video, which was Saul's pet name for me. But why would the old man want to leak this clip and make me look bad to the public? So no one would believe me if I uncovered his shadow project? And how had he come across that exact portion of the tapes? Had he searched the security archives for hours and hours just to find something incriminating? Or did he sit up there in his dark tower, watching us constantly and remembering everything we said?

"Thank you, Tara," I said, getting up to leave. "You've been a big help."

She put her hands on the fronts of my thighs as they were rising, and gently pushed them back down onto the chair. Then she leaned close.

"Michael, losing your daughter has got to be so hard for you," she said softly, but with a slight gleam in her eye where there should have been a tear. "This is when you need me the most." She moved even closer. Her hands still rested on my legs, and now our knees were touching. "Everyone will understand, with what you're going through and all."

"Lynn won't understand," I said, my mouth going dry. Tara bristled visibly, which made me feel bad because I was making her feel bad. This was the merry-go-round I couldn't seem to get off—I knew that I needed to finalize this, for the good of us all. But I couldn't bring myself to do it, because I feared hurting her. And there was also that motivation I had finally admitted to myself, that I liked the fact that she was waiting for me. She was just such a perfect specimen of a woman—physically, at least—only an object to me, yes, but almost overpowering in her raw appeal. Then again, that was exactly what Lynn was not—an object. Lynn was my friend, and the mother of my little girl. . . .

The thought of Lynette caused the anger to flare again, and once again it distracted me from the other feelings that were flowing. I reached down to pull Tara's hands off me, but when I lifted them, she managed to clasp them together with mine. I didn't want to jerk them apart, so now, despite my best efforts, we were holding hands in public.

"Don't you have another man, after all this time?" I asked, not knowing where else to go.

"I've had many, actually," she answered. "But they're not you." She squeezed my hands and leaned closer. "I know you can never forget me."

"That may be, but—" A tech walked by near us, holding

his head rigidly straight in a rather conspicuous manner. "Could I have my hands back, Tara?" She bristled again, but let go.

You cannot have my hands because they don't belong to you, I should have said. *You will never have my hand or any part of me again. It's over. Forever. If you have to get another job, get another job. Maybe I will.* But I didn't say that, gutless fool that I am. Instead, I tried to take the sting out of it for her, and added, "This isn't the place for that, right?"

She sat back in her chair and assumed a more professional demeanor.

"I relive that night last year over and over again," she said. "It was great, even though it was missing one important thing."

We had gone out to dinner and caught half a concert at Golden Gate Park, spending most of the time talking on the steps of one of the nearby museums. She had asked me out many times before, and I always had an excuse to say no, but for some reason that night I had agreed to go with her. When she wanted to drive me to her place rather than back to the castle, however, I told her it was too late, and she said if I kept telling her no, then someday it *might* be too late. I had to actually open the door and step out of the car a couple of blocks from the castle and walk the rest of the way, because she seemed unable to bring herself to drop me off there.

"Tara," I said, leaning forward and pushing my chair back a little. *It's over. It's over. That means it's over. O-V-E-R. Don't talk to me again, don't wait for me. I love my wife. . . .* "I have so much on my mind right now," was what I actually said. "We need to talk sometime. But now is not the time." I pushed myself up and out of the chair before she could intervene, and took a step away.

"Okay, let's talk," she said hopefully.

I cleared my throat, nodded, and walked away, determined not to look back.

I hit the nearest elevator and headed for the Confinement Center. On my way, I made a few calls to put the finishing touches on the Red Tunnel assault plan, priming a veritable army of bugs, falcons, mirrored tanks, and armored peacers who were now either on call or already in position.

As I rode the underground walkway connecting the castle to its neighboring building, I looked up at the cathedral through the transteel ceiling, which was reflective on the other side, providing more light at night for the courtyard on the surface. The charcoal-gray towers and reliefs of the old Gothic building were even more impressive from this far down—the view serving as a reminder to BASS employees about how lucky they were, and where they could end up if they ever crossed their employer . . . like I was planning to do.

The private conference room where I met Korcz was well inside the cathedral, but not as far as the cells themselves, which were in the very center, stretching down about ten stories below the ground. The husky, pockmarked man looked sober and worried, but I could tell he was glad to be free of the isolation of his cubicle, even though he'd only been in for less than a day. Saul Rabin's philosophy of incarceration differed significantly from the conventional wisdom that had developed during the last century, where inmates were allowed to live together in increasingly comfortable environments. The Mayor, on the other hand, thought that jail should be a place where one did *not* want to go, or stay. This retro-historical approach had caught on with a few of the new prisons here in the West, to which we happily sent the criminals who dared to defy any of our rules or simply needed a longer lesson.

"No one has told me anything." Korcz spoke first, his Euro-Russian accent muffled just slightly by the porous transteel wall between us. He wore a big bandage behind his ear, where my stopper had hit him. "I do not know why I am here. I do not know when I am leafing."

"Shouldn't you say 'if' you are leaving?" I said. "You did resist arrest. Under city law, as you well know, we could have killed you when you drew your guns."

"*If* I am leafing, then," he said. "Am I leafing?"

"*If* you answer a few questions, yes."

"I will try," he said warily, and my wheels started turning, wondering if I could get the information I wanted without tipping my hand to Big Brother. There were more cameras here in the cathedral than in the castle, most of them hidden. *The old man could be watching me now,* I thought; *or come across anything I say in his voyeuristic tape reviews.* Fortunately, I could act like I was investigating D's murder, which to any observer would reinforce the impression that I was still in the dark about it.

"Darien Anthony died two nights ago," I said. "Did you know that?"

"Yes," he answered. "But only on the plane here. I saw on the news."

"Did you think that had something to do with your arrest, when it was happening?"

"Indirectly," he said. "I never would have thought that I was a suspect, but I did fear that without him my past was . . . ah, how do you say it . . . catching up on me."

"Your crime had been forgiven," I reminded him.

"Perhaps by Darien . . . ah, Mr. Anthony. But not everyone at BASS is so merciful."

"Mr. Anthony's decision was official," I said.

"Perhaps, but an official decision is not necessarily a final one, danyet?" He looked up. "That can only come from the top."

"Why would you think our executive officers would be that capricious?" I included Paul in the question to obscure the fact that I wanted Korcz's opinion of his father. The bandaged man shrugged.

"I heard too many things when I was here, and saw a few, too. There is something rotten on this hill." He looked around and then looked back at me. "Maybe you are the one who stinks, ah? I thought it was higher than Anthony—but now you *are* higher than Anthony. Heh."

"I ask this because I'm still having trouble buying your supposed motives for running," I said, not really for Korcz but for any possible observers. "But tell me further about why you're so paranoid about the leaders here."

"I heard rumors, some from good sources, about plans that

were made"—he pressed on the bandage, as if he was afraid it might fall off—"to do something to us that only devils would do."

I felt the tingling sensation in my spine that happened only once in a while, when an interrogation was about to become something other than a total waste of time.

"What on earth could that possibly be?" I said, trying to sound incredulous and condescending.

"Some wetware shadow op with the smocks here in the church," he said, "so they could torque with our brains."

"Oh really," I said with a sarcastic tone and a slight smile. "I suppose this conspiracy had a secret name."

"I am not sure," he answered, irritated at my indifference. "But I heard it was called ROM 717." This was curious: Paul had said it was called Mind Lift. But I was glad for anything that might lead me to more information than I had been able to get so far.

"ROM seven one seven? Like read-only memory?"

"Maybe," Korcz said. "But from what I heard, I think it's from, ah . . . we call it 'beebliyah'?"

"The Bible?" I asked, and he nodded. *Not again,* I thought initially, but then realized that this information was probably legit, because it seemed to fit with what I had heard from Kim and D's Twotter file about the religious undercurrent in the "first family."

"So then ROM 717 would mean . . . what?" I asked, careful to seem bored and amused rather than genuinely interested.

"Do I look like someone who reads books like that?" he asked, and I thought, *I don't know what you would look like. Saul*

Rabin doesn't look like that kind of person. "But I would like to go now, please, before something like that happens to me."

"Korcz, listen to me," I said, leaning forward. "I don't believe this bloody fairy tale for one minute. And you shouldn't, either. I know the Rabins, and I know me, and we have nothing but the best in mind for our personnel." I sat back up, admiring my next move. "Just to show you how harmless and gracious we are, you can leave right now with your record wiped clean."

He stared at me, then glanced to the left and right briefly.

"Go on," I concluded, standing up to leave. "Tell your parents we're sorry for what happened. And have a nice vacation."

I wore the glasses through the security checks on the way out, issuing the final mobilization orders for the assault forces. Twitch was on duty again, excited about another chance to exercise his new falcon command, but also eager to be the first to employ the prototype bugs in an actual combat situation. His enthusiasm was contagious—I found myself forgetting all about Lynette, Lynn, Tara, and the old man as I high-stepped through the elevators to the staging sight, looking forward to releasing some of the aggression pent up inside me.

"Just between me and you, sir," the young falconer said to me, though we both knew that other agents were on the line. "The Red Tunnel should have been cleaned out a long time ago."

"Just between me and you, Twitch," I said, "I hope they resist arrest."

10

It felt good to be involved in a military operation again, for the first time in many years, and I found the preparations for battle especially cathartic. Sitting a hundred feet under Divisadero Street in the part of the Red Tunnel that the squatters hadn't taken, watching the men and machines deploy at various locations on the bank of screens in front of me, I remembered Taiwan. The adrenaline now was just a trickle compared to the rush back then, but it felt good anyway. There is less excitement when you know you're going to win a fight, but on the other hand, the absence of any real fear heightens the pleasure considerably.

On the way to the tunnel, I had stopped at a net room, where I offered several major media outlets the first rights to information going what was going to happen, in exchange for their promise to air something I gave to them as a part of their reports.

I changed into clothes that were semibulletproof (but looked basically the same), and moved the boas to the front and switched them so that the killer was now ready for my right hand. This was only in case something went desperately wrong, which was highly unlikely. The squatters were severe underdogs, if they even resisted us, but sometimes the worst odds could be beaten.

Twitch's leg was shaking feverishly again as he put the finishing touches on the bug prep. The tiny flying cameras were our latest innovation in the Sabon antigravity technology, and this was their first serious real-life test, which was one reason why I didn't have them loaded with explosives, though I would have liked to. I also needed Harris and his home intact so that I could get rid of the evidence in my datafold in the way I had planned. Gassing the whole place had been ruled out for the same reason, plus the fact that I was concerned about a negative reaction from the public. This way would be much better for PR, especially if they put up a fight.

"Okay, we're ready," Twitch said finally, and looked at me, his leg still vibrating. I nodded, and he touched his handpad, diving into cyberspace. His leg and the rest of his body became still, as did the other members of his team, and some of the screens came alive with swirling sample images from the bugs. I couldn't make out their locations by looking at the screens, because the images shook so violently, but I knew that more than five hundred of them were entering the tunnel's delta through five different air ducts. They separated and swept through the entire delta in a matter of minutes, transmitting everything they scanned back to the mainframe, which collated the data and organized it into a "report" that soon appeared on the screen bank and in the glasses of the many agents waiting at various points around the squatters.

"How did we do?" I asked a tech near me as Twitch transitioned slowly back into reality.

"Forty-three percent redundancy, and about fifty of them died before full reel, so we're far from optimal. But the composite picture is good. We know what it looks like in there, and we know where their weapons are."

I told him to show me, and soon a screen in front of me displayed a depiction of the big central room of the delta, as if I were walking through it. The new residents had left the thick red lines on the floor and walls (hence "Red Tunnel") and surrounded them with bizarre graffiti. They had also added makeshift rooms on the outside, the walls of which could be identified because they had graffiti but no red lines. Each squatter figure that came into view in my virtual stroll was frozen motionless, but some were adorned with flashing red lights, superimposed by the software, which announced that they were armed. There was also a big clump of red spots on the wall of one of the makeshift rooms I passed, indicating that a stash of weapons was stored somewhere inside of it.

"Show me Harris's lair," I said, and the view began to fast-forward through the big room, until it came to gaze upon one wall, which was completely transparent, making it the best feat of engineering the squatters had accomplished. On the other side of the transteel was Harris, sitting in the middle of what looked like a computer junkyard. Screens were all around him, but lower in the front and on the left so that he could see out through the wall and greet visitors who came through the door to the room, which was on the left. The red blips told me that he had at least two guns in there with him.

I left the virtual image on the screen, imagining Harris in his room, and had the tech dial him.

"My precious!" said the freak, he and his tattoos appearing live on another screen. "What in Mary's Armpit was that?"

"That was our newest toy," I answered. "A swarm of plasteel insects that scanned your entire hideout before you could blink. As I'm sure you know, the Eye is not as effective as usual because you're underground. But thanks to the bugs, we now know every inch of this potential battleground better than you do, and the exact quantity and nature of your ordnance, so I'd like to suggest—one time only—that you surrender immediately to the BASS forces gathered outside your cityside entrance."

Please say no, I thought.

"You want me to say no, I can tell," Harris said, appearing thoughtful for a moment, until he showed me his dental artwork again in an exaggerated smile. "You gave me a not-so-Distant Early Warning, so let me return the favor. If you huff and puff and blow our doors down, I guarantee you will regret it. We will broadcast the whole Shebang, and you *will* have some casualties. And if you strike me down, I will become more powerful than you can possibly imagine. Better just *let it be, let it be, let it be, yeah, let it be . . .*" He went on singing, but I could tell that underneath the bravado, he was afraid, like a bill he couldn't pay had finally come due. But his comment about casualties did make me wonder how he was planning to accomplish that. He was just crazy and smart enough to have something up his sleeve.

"Well, in that case, maybe we should talk some more," I said and went on to ask him a question. But as I did, I showed Twitch and the nearby commander two fingers, which had the effect of moving the team of puppeteers into cyberspace and the rest of our forces into their final positions. All the screens around the image of Harris lit up with a menagerie of views from birds and men, and when I saw the commander hold out three of his fingers, I met them with four of my own, and suddenly the screens went from motionless to manic. Some flashed brightly as a number of closed-off passages around the perimeter of the delta were blasted open, including the blocked part of the main tunnel that led into it. The noise of that big blast drowned out the smaller ones, especially since we were closest to it, and the earth shook hard for a few seconds.

Harris immediately clicked off when he heard it, so I was able to watch the screens as I slipped my glasses on and imported the three or four that I thought would give me the best overview of the action.

Through each of the five new holes in the outer walls of the delta shot a falcon and then two peacers, camouflaged by the clouds of smoke and dust caused by the blasts. These squads moved through the tributary hallways, following directions predetermined by the bug data, firing stopper rounds at anything that moved, and throwing "bore bombs" at every closed door. These were golf-ball-size grenades that attached to whatever surface they hit, then burned through to the other side and sprayed that room with a knockout gas that was undaunted by most masks known to man.

Through the section of the tunnel that had been cleared, and into the big central room, rolled a small fleet of custom "tunnel tanks," as we had called them during the preparations for the op. Each of the minivan-size vehicles held four gunmen and a pilot, completely surrounded by an armored shell that was transparent from the inside but mirrored on the outside. Their guns poked through flexible patches of the mirrored armor, so that they could easily see and shoot anyone on their side of the tank, while their opponents were being disoriented by the reflections of themselves and other parts of their environment. When the squatters who were armed did manage to fire at the tanks, their low-tech bullets and shells were easily repelled by the armor. The mirrored surfaces also prevented the use of lasers.

The feed I was watching most during the battle was one from inside a tank, looking over the shoulder of a gunman. I found the lopsided turkey shoot quite satisfying, especially when a long stream of stoppers from his big rifle laid waste to a hastily erected barricade, and then reached the squatters who had been shooting from behind it. It was unlikely that they would survive the hail, because so many of the rubbery Xs had hit them before the gunman moved on to his next target. Looking beyond the immediate scene, I briefly made out one of the other tanks, which looked like a shimmering blur as it raced along the outside of the big room, firing more bore bombs at the doors of the rooms the squatters had built there.

Then the tank I was in turned in a different direction, bouncing up and down as it ran over something solid, which might or might not have been a body. The gunman drew a bead on some fleeing squatters, but he let them go when he saw that they were headed for the cityside exit. They would be picked up by the small army we had waiting out there. The tank turned again, ran over something or someone again, and I caught a glimpse of Harris sitting in the room with the transparent wall. He hadn't moved from his seat in the middle of the equipment, but now there were two armed figures near the door to protect him.

That was when the first squad got hit with the NuPain.

One of the views in my glasses belonged to an unlucky peacer, and I noticed out of the corner of my eye that his faceplate camera was suddenly pointed down, then in various directions, as if he was shaking his head violently. His audio line was not open to me, but I imagined his screams of pain. I read the squad number on the bottom right of his view, and said to the editor, "Give me the bird on two."

Within seconds, the view from a falcon replaced the others and filled the inside of my glasses, placing me at the scene and hitting me with a generous dose of the usual sensation of vertigo. It was worse than usual, because the falcon was moving excessively, swinging around and up and down as if its pilot wasn't sure what to do. Through the dizzying waves, however, I was able to register the scene: the squad was in a hallway they had been cleaning, but rather than moving through it efficiently, the two men were now stopped in their tracks, one standing and the other kneeling, but both clutching the sides of their necks. Their guns were on the floor near them, as was a small, smoking hole where one had dropped a grenade.

The man on his knees fell to his face, twitching, and the other one pulled off his faceplate as he stood, staggering. He seemed to be wearing shadows on his ears and below them, and as I watched, the black spread quickly onto his cheeks. The falcon dipped down toward him, so that his contorted face filled my vision. The encroaching darkness on it was something like a burn, but not really. It looked like some kind of cancer, spreading at an accelerated rate.

I heard the commander behind me tell the falcon's controller to scan the fallen peacer, and it did, revealing that he was no longer breathing. By the time the bird had swung back around, his partner was on the ground, too. At that point, the falcon sprayed both of their heads with foam, starting with the one that was still alive. This measure was designed to stop bleeding and burns, but there was no way of knowing if it would have any effect in this case, because none of us knew what was happening.

As the falcon moved close to the dead man to attempt to revive him, I saw one of the other squads approaching up the hallway, and asked for the line to them.

"Proceed with caution," I said, and they slowed. "Send the falcon ahead at lead distance." The bird from the new squad pulled away from them, and I switched my view into it. I was telling Twitch to sweep the hall thoroughly when another squad, elsewhere in the delta, encountered the same problem. I received the feed from their falcon, but minimized it to a small corner of the glasses so that I didn't have to endure the same horror again. This time, both men immediately jerked to the floor in pain.

I was about to tell all squads to hold their positions, when two voices started screaming in my ears. I said Twitch's name, and he turned the falcon, which had been studying the walls and doors, back toward the relief squad, which had slowly crept up to their fallen comrades, only to be waylaid with the same disease. I turned the glasses' audio off, too slowly, but then noticed that one of the dying men was pointing forward and up as he sank to his knees. His blackening mouth was moving, so I switched the audio back on.

". . . From the light," he croaked, then exhaled a death rattle and went the rest of the way to the floor, completing the pile of four bodies.

"All squads hold position," I said, then told Twitch to continue to attempt to revive the men, and turned to the commander and the tech standing beside him. "Some kind of gas our scan didn't pick up." They agreed by nodding. "Short-range delivery, only to certain locations." They agreed again. "The two squads left should hold their positions. Send two back-up squads into this location, but only by the route that has already been covered. Stop at thirty feet out."

By the time the backups had moved into position, it became obvious that neither shock nor chemical treatment was going to bring the fallen men back. So, when the teams arrived at the scene, I ordered the two falcons already there to move apart from each other, but within range of the big rectangular light set into the ceiling. Then I sent the new bird in to do a close-up scan of the light. It floated into a position almost directly under it, but a few feet away.

"There's a square outline to the right of the light," I said as I looked through the middle falcon. "Zoom in on that." I maximized the view until it filled my glasses, so I could see more detail. The small square grew larger slowly as the falconer followed my order, until it filled my view and did appear to be some kind of closed flap. As I was studying it, the flap suddenly slid open and the barrel of a large handgun, held by a small hand, poked through the hole. The black hole at the end of its muzzle filled my view, and then flashed as it shot me right in the face. I winced, mashing my eyes closed and hearing the sounds of the shots and their impact on the bird from the open line to the backup squads. When I opened my eyes again, my view had automatically defaulted to one of the other two falcons, and I watched the rest of the skirmish from that bird's-eye view.

The remaining two falcons began firing at the extended hand and gun, hitting the ceiling and light next to it. Surprisingly, the light stayed on for a few seconds, and the hand retracted momentarily. It reappeared in the middle of the barrage and tossed an object the size of a fat pill toward the men in the back-up squads. As we shouted at them to fall back, they did, apparently far enough that the timed discharge of gas didn't reach them.

Meanwhile, the falcons made short work of the assailant. They had to use killer rounds to make sure they penetrated the ceiling and the light's casing, and they didn't stop firing until the still-extended hand was obviously hanging limp, the gun having fallen to the floor. The falcons' spotlights now shone on the shattered remains of the light, because the hallway had grown considerably darker without it.

We were deciding on our next move when the riddled light casing creaked loudly and then collapsed with the crash of glass, metal, and ceiling board. All that, plus a small, bloody body, rained down to the floor between the two floating birds. Their cameras and lights turned toward the pile, and we then saw that the guerrilla was a little boy, probably about ten years old, with blood covering much of his body, and tattoos on the rest of it. He was naked except for a leather belt with a few pouches hanging from it.

I had known that there were children living among the squatters, whom they had "adopted" (read *corrupted*). But I had failed to notice that very few of the children had been visible in the earlier stages of the operation. This could have meant that they were locked up inside rooms, but it could also have meant that the squatters had armed them and stuck them in ambush positions in the moments right after our bugs had swept the delta.

I cursed myself for having given them a warning, as I studied the hole in the ceiling through the falcon's camera. I could see why they used the children: the space above the light was not big enough for an adult, especially with extra support built into it. I guessed that someone in the slot could see down into the hallway, but no one could see him, which also made it ideal for this purpose.

As I thought of how many other, similar ambushes might await us throughout the delta, it occurred to me that if we hadn't staggered the pacing of the squads and we hadn't stopped them when we had, we might have lost every one of them, plus quite a few backups. It was even possible that we might have cut our losses and retreated. It amazed me to think that Harris actually could have pulled this off, and that he still might give us some trouble. I may have actually felt some grudging admiration for the walking work of art, but mostly I was even more eager to kill him.

11

All the squads were still holding and doing fine, so I took this opportunity to back up each of them, to check the progress of the tanks in the big room, and to allow some more time for the gas in the hallway to dissipate. We had already concluded, however, that it had a very brief life span.

When I thought we had waited long enough, I sent one squad ahead, farther into the hallway, imagining their hearts beating faster as they faced the prospect of meeting their doom if the chemical was still active. But the gas was gone, as we had thought, and they were even able to pull a few remaining pellets out of the dead boy's pouch. The peacer who examined them told us they were triggered by an Ehrlich mechanism. To activate it, the user had to grasp the pellet between finger and thumb, depressing both ends for three seconds. Then the gas would discharge in another three seconds. These kinds of "immediate action" weapons were reserved for people like jihadists who placed very little value on even their own lives . . . you had to be very desperate or even suicidal to use them.

We went back into the virtual tunnel to see how many lengths of hallway had yet to be cleaned, and also to try to pick out any signs of other ambush spots. Believe it or not, some of the bugs had recorded such a high level of detail that we could actually zoom in and see little squares next to the lights in a few other sections of hallway. So now we knew where some of the other prepubescent assassins were—if the squatters had chosen to use those compartments.

"We have another fleet of bugs, right?" I asked Twitch, who seemed shaken by the situation, perhaps because he had just witnessed six painful deaths from an intimately close perspective. He said, "Yes, sir," and I told him to send in five at a time, one for each member of his puppeteer team, and scour the ceilings until they located all possible dangers. So the falconers left their birds hanging where they were, on autopilot, and began an hour-long process of scanning the hallways. It took so long because new bugs had to be employed every few minutes. Their tiny antigrav engines were not able to last any longer, at this early stage in their development.

Long before the bugs were done with their task, the tanks had finished theirs. They had completely cleared the big room at the end of the delta, and the two that had not been assigned to moving patrol were sitting near Harris's office, facing the freak and his two bodyguards, who were safe for now behind the impenetrable see-through wall. Harris was still sitting in the same place amid his equipment, but he was gesticulating wildly as he broadcast what he undoubtedly thought was a PR nightmare for BASS.

I so looked forward to enlightening him with the truth, but I had to sit tight until the hallways were cleared.

That happened with more of a whimper than a bang, as the falcons assaulted the pinpointed danger spots one after another, firing gas pellets through the flaps, after we'd found out that would work. The peacers would then pull the unconscious children out of their slots, relieving them of their lethal toys. We missed only one, because she was hidden in a wall slot behind a couple of movie posters. One man died before we realized what was happening, but so did the little girl, when his partner reacted instinctively and blew open the wall with a grenade from his rifle, before the falcon could gas her. As I watched the tail end of this mess, I thought of Lynette, who was not that much younger than the girl, and the aggression inside me boiled to a rage.

Shortly after that, even though the hallways were not yet completely cleared, I ordered a team to enter the big room through the cityside gate, which we had secured at the very beginning of the op. As I watched from a camera inside one of the tanks that was facing Harris's room, they crept alongside the wall to the left of it, unseen by anyone inside. When they reached the heavy transparent door on the left end of the room, I told the commander to give them the signal to take it.

The point man placed two matchbox light bombs on the wall near him, which immediately sped across the door and onto the transteel wall, until they stopped at a spot directly in front of Harris and his two bodyguards. From their bottoms, the little robots discharged a glaring pulse of light through the wall that temporarily but very thoroughly blinded the men. Within seconds our team was inside the room, disarming Harris and his buddies, though one of the peacers was wounded by the rounds that Harris fired wildly toward the door. He also hit one of his own men, but that didn't prove to be fatal, either.

Part of the assault team hauled the bodyguards and wounded agent away, while the rest searched the room thoroughly for booby traps. But they left Harris where he was, as I had instructed, and posted a guard. After they were done, I checked the status of the hallway clean-up to make sure it was going well, then slid my boas to the front of my belt and walked into the tunnel, ignoring the concerned pleas of a pilot who had kept his tank in the command area so that I could ride it into the combat area. That would have been safer, for sure, but my blood was up from watching the assault and I wanted to enter the fray to some degree at least. The tank followed me as I strode through the smoking debris, broken bodies, and cases of spent ammunition that littered the hallways (the last was from the squatters' weapons, because we used caseless ammo). I reached the big room without incident, which was somewhat of a disappointment, and the pilot of the tank shadowing me parked it next to the other two that were facing the transteel wall. I headed into Harris's office, leaving the big door open and motioning for the guard to leave.

"Are those guns, or are you just glad to see me?" the multi-colored man said, with a fake laugh. He looked smaller in person, and sickly—maybe because he knew the end was near. I noticed that the chair he sat in wasn't just a chair but his bed, bathroom, and kitchen as well. There were intravenous and other tubes connected to his lower abdomen, and I could tell from looking at the room that it had formerly been one of the delta's bathrooms. He had obviously chosen this one because the plumbing system was already there, ready to connect to his chair. I had heard about hologame cultists who lived this way (never leaving one spot), but it surprised me that Harris did it, until I realized that it made perfect sense for someone whose entire life was the net.

"Did you like our little surprise?" he asked. I nodded, and asked him what it was.

"I *knew* you never would have cataloged it," he said, all but patting himself on the back. "It's an old thing from the Russian civil war. Don't know what it was called there, but the people who brought it over called it NuPain—with a *u*. Don't usually do business with that bunch of phobes, but I had to have it. How many less agents does the BigASS have now?"

I ignored his question and, knowing there was no BASS surveillance in here, went straight to the point.

"I want you to tell me anything you know about a BASS black op designed to control people through neuroware in their brains," I said. "And maybe I'll spare your worthless life." He tilted his head in puzzlement, since he was expecting me to gloat or lash out—anything but ask him a question.

"I have to think for a while," he said, striking the pose from the famous Greek statue.

"No, just tell me if you know anything. Our conversations are over, except for any information you might have on that topic."

Something in my voice made him grow very serious, suddenly looking like a different person.

"I heard something like that years ago when I was there," he said. "But I really don't know any more about it. I wish . . . I wish I did."

I decided against pursuing it any further and told him to turn on the news. "Just search for your name," I added. "I'm sure you'll find something."

Looking more puzzled, and even fearful now, Harris did as I'd said. Soon his search program found an entry, and brought up a newscast on a screen to his left. One of the talking heads he despised so much was telling the Bay Area and the world the same thing that would be broadcast a million times over on the infinite Net:

". . . The downfall of a popular Web figure from the San Francisco Bay Area. Harold Harris, former employee of the company who rules that part of the world, became the darling hero of many by playing counterrevolutionary in BASS's backyard, and a fascinating curiosity for many more by sending out waves of slick netfare from his pilfered palace. For two years, he has projected an air of moral superiority, claiming that a corrupt BASS has a callous disregard for human life, while he and his friends are standing for a sublime ideal of human rights.

"BASS authorities have broken their long silence about Harris and his fellow 'squatters,' as they are called in the city. Michael Ares, an executive agent in the company, released a statement today saying that after repeated attempts to peacefully persuade the squatters to return their stolen property, the time has come for a forceful eviction. To show that Harris is not the philanthropist or saint that he makes himself out to be, Ares also released a vidclip, certified by Reality G and three federal agencies, which proves that the squatter was responsible for injuries sustained by innocent people in a recent arrest . . ."

They went on to show the conversation between Harris and me about the Korcz incident, which the tech named Kim had recorded by skillfully beating the squatters' blocks. It made clear to the watching world that if anyone had a "callous disregard for human life," it was Harris. Especially when it ended like this:

Me: "You realize people could have been killed or wounded."

Harris: "Torque 'em! That would have been Even Better Than the Real Thing."

"Singing about the death of innocents?" the talking head on the news concluded. "If anyone questioned the legitimacy of evicting the squatters, those questions are gone now. And if any of us questioned the truth of Harris's bold claims, we are now sure that he cannot be trusted."

The news went on to another topic, but Harris left it on, staring at the screen and silently processing the effect this had on his career as a crusader, not to mention what being in jail without the net would do to his soul. I hoped he was thinking hard as I lifted the palm-size disk in my hand to where he could see it out of the corner of his eye. To the underside of the explosive, which was very similar to the one that had killed D and Lynette, I had attached the little disk containing the incriminating picture of me.

"This bomb is about to blow all your best friends into a thousand pieces," I said, waving it at the piles of equipment. "Once I drop it, you have ten seconds to leave with me for a cyberless cell, or you can stay here and beat me to hell."

He didn't say anything, but just stared at the news, where the weather was currently being discussed.

I slid the trigger on the disk in three different directions until it was primed, then bowled it across a length of bare floor, much like I had done the other night at my friend's house, while my daughter was saying hi to me from the backseat.

I turned and stepped to the door, looking back one more time to see if Harris was coming. He wasn't, as I had expected, so I closed the door and walked at a normal pace toward my tank. When I had almost reached it, I looked at the mirrored surface of the vehicle and saw Harris sitting inside his room, staring at the screen. Then there was a fiery flash that filled the room and struck my eyes through the reflection, so bright that I was forced to close them. But not before I saw my own figure in the reflection, silhouetted against the bright glow of the blast, just like in the image I had now destroyed.

I opened my eyes again, and still looking at the reflection on the tank, I studied the big transteel wall, which had stood strong in the blast, as I had known it would. Its inside was covered with dark shards of metal and plastic that had been propelled into it by the force of the blast, interspersed with dripping patches of bloody flesh.

I was dismayed to find that my anger wasn't gone, and now I felt sick and sweaty, too, like I needed a shower.

I turned toward the cityside exit and headed for it.

"Is there a bookstore near here?" I asked an officer at the gate. I needed to find out more about the old man's secret project but was too paranoid to use the net and leave any kind of cyber-print related to it.

"I don't know, sir, sorry," he said. "Why do you ask?"

"I need to get some religion," I answered, and stepped out into the streets of San Francisco.

12

It was starting to get dark as I wove through the crowd that had gathered around our barricades on the surface, outside the entrance to the tunnel, and the city assailed my senses.

I supposed the people who lived here were immune to the sights, sounds, and smells of this metropolis, but they always hit me like I was running into a wall. My eyes immediately tended to twirl and glaze from the unfamiliar stimuli of a thousand moving parts and the scale of the surrounding buildings. My ears almost hurt at the cacophony of voices, vehicles, and video advertisements, both flat and holo, that were being projected onto the streets and sidewalks. And the rotation of strong aromas could only be described as bittersweet—an unpleasant residue from the chemical products (natural and not-so-natural) of a million sardined humans, punctuated with refreshing bursts of sea air blowing in from the Bay.

I seldom left a controlled environment, and this was anything but. I knew that Lynn and probably Paul would have thrown fits if they'd known what I was doing. They would have told me that I was recognizable, and would be afraid that some anti-BASS gang of thugs would dismember me before the cavalry could show up. But my state of mind right now was such that I really didn't care, and I needed to be outside the reach of BASS surveillance to do what I wanted to do.

As I studied some of the faces I passed in the crowd, however, the fear seemed unfounded. Very few recognized me (at least noticeably), none approached, and most simply went about their business, not on the lookout for famous people by any means. After all, I was the least well known of the BASS executives: the old man was a living legend, Paul was his son, and D had been our charismatic, smiling face for the media. I had hardly ever appeared on the net by choice, and the tabloid coverage had focused mostly on those three.

Nevertheless, a few people did recognize me as I walked a few blocks up Powell Street. And a woman I asked about a bookstore noticed at least one of the boas, because the breeze had blown my jacket open while I was talking to her. I closed it partially then to avoid scaring too many people, but I left the guns in front in case I met anyone that I *needed* to scare.

I turned a corner, looking for the Noble Virgin. The woman had said, "Can't miss it," and she was right. It took up half a block along this street, almost the entire first floor of a typically colossal building that stretched so high that I couldn't see the top from this angle. I stepped in and noticed that the buzz of noise was even louder in here than on the street. This was from the conversations going on at the coffeehouses on the perimeter of the huge floor, but also from the many sampling and downloading stations spread throughout it—not that the various media itself was so loud, but people experiencing it through earphones, glasses, goggles, and headgear always tended to talk louder to their friends, as if they were hard of hearing.

I had barely stepped inside the door when I was greeted by three tense security guards and a smiling customer-service representative, or manager (he was not wearing an ID tag). The boas had undoubtedly been scanned and set off a silent alarm. The man recognized me immediately, and said my name, at which the guards relaxed considerably. I gave him a card, which he dutifully ran through his Reality G terminal as the guards continued to watch me dutifully.

He came back and returned my card. "It's good to have you here, Mr. Ares," he said in a low voice, to avoid any more attention than was already being lavished on me by some onlookers. "Is there anything we can help you with?" He motioned the guards away, and they reluctantly left. So did the gawkers.

"Actually, there is," I said, hesitating to make what I was doing public, but not knowing any other way to find what I was looking for. "I want to find something in the Bible."

"Okay," he said, trying not to look surprised. "Veel or real?"

"Well, it was written as a real book, right? So I guess I want to see one of those." What I really wanted was to stay away from any media where there might be a record of what I was doing.

"Oh," he said, nodding. "So are you referring to the Old Bible?" When he saw my puzzled look, he explained. "There are . . . I forget the exact number right now, but . . . thousands of different versions of that book. Everything from obscure, homemade holos to the bestselling *Open Scriptures* done by top religious scholars. Most of them are in a virtual format, of course, though there are some real ones. But we have a collector's item called the Old Bible—only a few of them in print, because there's not much demand—that is actually translated into English right from the ancient languages, like they used to do."

"So that's the . . . *true* version?" I asked.

"What is 'true,' Mr. Ares?" he answered, shrugging his shoulders and smirking. "But some people—'purists' would be one of the nicer names for them—do think so." He glanced around for a moment, as if he were looking for someone. "Would you like to see one of those? We usually don't bring them out, because they're so expensive, but for you I will."

"Okay," I said, and he began to lead me through the maze of stations to a back corner of the store, where the smaller selection of "real books" was kept. On the way, I saw hundreds of people of all ages sampling or buying audio, video, and holo media, by downloading it into their OutPhones, InPhones, goggles, glasses, or personal "pockets" so that they could carry it home to their net rooms. The first and last were the ubiquitous choices of most consumers at this time, because implants and goggles that worked consistently were still quite expensive, and good glasses were even more. The cyber-pocket boom started with video and game pockets (known as "vips" and "gaps"), then developed into holo pockets ("hops"), then culminated recently in all-media pockets, or "amps," which every human being from age four up now considered one of the basic necessities of life.

There was a time not long before when it looked like all media would become downloadable by terminals at home or other wireless receptors like those mentioned above, which would have made stores like this obsolete and put them out of business. But before that could happen, the big retail companies conglomerated and made deals with the media producers to pay higher prices for the exclusive rights to their properties, and then began to charge even higher prices to the consumers, who couldn't buy them anywhere else . . . an example of how capitalism was still alive and well in the West, despite the socialist experimentation of the last generation (or maybe because of it).

As we finally passed into the real-books part of the store, the buzz of noise instantly disappeared and was replaced by the hum of soft music, so that the customers reading at various tables and cubicles throughout the section could concentrate. Obviously the store was using an invisible sound barrier, like the ones we had throughout the castle where our employees had offices in or near busy floors. And not only was the atmosphere different, but the people in here were generally another breed. They were those who had enough intellectual and cultural interest to reach this back part of the store, having pressed through the gauntlet of the more popular distractions along the way. I wondered if some of them might be a part of the small but growing movement of intellectuals who protested "the scourge of modern media" by reading *only* real books. It occurred to me that Lynn would be a good candidate for that movement, if she had been inclined toward activism (which she was not) or considered herself an intellectual (which she did not).

My guide ushered me to a table near a transparent case containing antique and collectible volumes, then proceeded to open it with his key card. He pulled out a book with a cordovan leather cover that sagged down around his fingers as he carried it over and put it in front of me.

"Be careful," he said, "the pages are very thin."

I opened it and noticed that they were indeed, then asked him about ROM 717. I regretted it immediately, feeling like I was hanging out dirty laundry. He gave me a blank stare, then said he would find out if any of the other employees knew about this sort of thing. "No, wait," I said, stopping him, an idea coming to me about someone who could help. "I'm fine, I'll take care of it."

"No problem," he quickly responded, moving away. "If there is anything else you need, just say 'service' into your amp, phone, or glasses, and our in-store line will pick it up."

When he was gone, I called Kim at the castle and asked him to come to the store as soon as he could get here, saying I had some questions about his religion. I couldn't ask him what I wanted to know over the net for fear of being overheard. Fortunately, the young tech was still at work and able to slip away. While I waited for him, I paged through the old book and wondered what all the fuss was about . . . the parts I saw didn't make much sense to me. I gave up well before Kim arrived and was checking messages on my glasses when he entered the real-books part of the store. He was sweating and panting from his haste to accommodate me, but when he saw the book sitting in front of me, he brightened and practically shivered with excitement. He wasn't wearing his cyber equipment, but I guessed it was in the small case he was carrying.

"I'm looking for something in here called ROM 717," I told him. "Whatever that is."

He thought for a moment, then swung around behind me, flipped a few pages, and pointed at a spot on one of them.

"I think you mean seven seventeen, sir, not seven one seven," he said proudly, "in the book of Romans." I looked at the words near his finger, which had the figure 17 in front of them. It said, "I am no longer the one doing it, but sin which indwells me."

"Yeah. That looks like the one," I said, then asked him what it meant.

"That's a good question," he said; and then, observing how I was craning my neck up to see him, he asked politely if he could sit down across from me. I said yes, and watched him do so. He still seemed very excited but was now trying not to show it too much.

"I thought this was a vision at first," the man said with his self-conscious smile. "But it's real." I directed a puzzled stare at him for a few moments, but then simply nodded my head twice. Then he asked, "Why did you want to find that verse, sir?"

I hesitated, thinking, *I'm investigating the murder of my daughter and best friend, which I myself committed.* But I answered, "A friend mentioned it to me. It may have some significance for something that's happening in my life. So I want to know everything I can about it."

"Well, that could take a while," he said, seeming even more excited. "But I can give you the short version."

I said that would be good.

"First, read the other verses around it, and you might be able to figure out a lot of it." I felt like a child in school, but did as he suggested.

> For that which I am doing, I do not understand; for I am not doing what I would like to do, but I am doing the very thing I hate. But if I do the very thing I do not want to do, I agree with the Law, confessing that it is good. So now, I am no longer the one doing it, but sin which indwells me. For I know that nothing good dwells in me, that is, in my flesh; for the wishing is present in me, but the doing of the good is not. For the good that I want to do, I do not do; but I practice the very evil that I do not want to do. But if I am doing the very thing I do not want to do, I am no longer the one doing it, but sin which dwells in me. I find then the principle that evil is present in me, the one who wishes to do good. For I joyfully agree with the law of God in the inner man, but I see a different law in the members of my body, waging war against the law of my mind, and making me a prisoner of the law of sin which is in my members. Wretched man

> that I am! Who will set me free from the body of this death? Thanks be to God through Jesus Christ our Lord . . .

"The guy is torn apart inside," I said, looking back up at Kim. "Something is making him to do what he doesn't want to do." The tech nodded, and I was realizing that old man Rabin must have picked this out from perusings in this book because it described the nature of his black op. Maybe he also thought it somehow gave credibility to what he was doing, but that didn't matter to me. And it didn't provide any help regarding a solution; Christ had been the deliverer for this ancient religious writer, but I couldn't expect any help from him.

"If Jesus knew how some people were using his Bible," I said to Kim, "he would roll over in his grave."

"But he's not in his grave," he responded too quickly, holding his breath in excitement (or maybe fear?). "He rose from the dead—that's how he can help us with our sins."

Oh boy, here we go, I thought, remembering the complaints I had heard about this variety of fundamentalists, that they insist on ramming their beliefs down everyone's throat. I was about to close the book and the discussion, but then a thought hit me and I looked down at one of the verses again. It reminded me of the internal struggle I had been having.

"Why does he call himself a wretched man," I asked, "when he never intended to commit the crime?" I started to regret the minor slip, but then relaxed when I realized it was likely that Kim cared more about his faith than my reasons for being here.

"Well, I can't remember what I've heard about that 'I'm not doing it' part," the tech said, thinking furiously. "But he does plenty of other things wrong, he's guilty for them at least, and he needs to be forgiven." He paused, and when I didn't cut him off, he went on. "We do what is wrong because of the evil in the world around us but also because of the evil that's *in* us, or else sin would have no appeal to us. But it does, and even when the evil is being done to us, we don't love our enemies in return like we should. So we're to blame no matter how you slice it, and we still need to be justified by God. Have you ever heard of justification?"

I didn't respond, because I was thinking how that might indeed be the reason I felt such guilt from what I had done, even though it had not been a conscious act. I had willfully chosen to live in the world of BASS, and I definitely did have hatred and murder brewing inside me as a result of my suffering.

"Justification is the best thing I ever learned about," Kim continued. "Being *justified is just as if I'd* never done wrong, and *just as if I'd* always done everything right. And we get it as a gift from God, by believing in Jesus, because he took our place on the cross. See . . ." He lowered his finger toward the page in front of me, as if he wanted me to read more, but I squinted and smiled at him.

"Are you trying to convert me to your thing?" I said.

He looked deflated for a moment, sinking back into his chair, then said, "I just get excited about it, sir. You see, I've done a lot of bad things . . . things like Mr. Anthony did with that woman. In the Twotter file, remember?" I nodded, remembering.

"In fact, that's how I met my wife, believe it or not." He exhaled sharply and looked away. "I'm just so glad that's all gone."

I was startled initially to hear the man confess this, because I had always thought that religious people lived a "clean life." I didn't think they visited prostitutes, nor did I think they would marry one, even if she was supposedly reformed. Then my mind drifted to D's womanizing, no doubt because Kim had mentioned him, and it occurred to me that I had taken pride in the fact that I was with either Tara or Lynn the whole time I had known him, and had not cheated on either of them. But now it also occurred to me that I was essentially no better than my friend, because I approved of his lifestyle and entertained similar thoughts in my own mind.

"Forgiven, you know?" Kim added. I told him that I understood, with a lack of conviction, but he seemed to perk up again anyway.

"Have you ever asked for forgiveness?" the devotee now blurted out, giving the impression that this was his final question, a last-ditch attempt to leave me with a little part of his belief. I felt like I should answer him, because I didn't want him to think that I was a prospect, or that I needed anything he was trying to offer me. So I made up something as I spoke, and tried to make it sound profound.

"Well, it seems to me that would be a sign of weakness," I said. "Saying you need forgiveness implies that you are at fault, and that you need someone else to affirm you or absolve you. Basically, you're putting yourself at the mercy of another and giving them a position of strength over you." I didn't feel any need to explain why this was so undesirable—my military and police background made it self-evident in my mind.

The tech looked at me for a moment, to make sure I was finished. I was, so I spread my hands slightly to elicit his response.

"I agree," was all that he said.

Then we heard the voice of the man who had met me at the door, who must have been watching us as he was approaching.

"Is everything okay, Mr. Ares?" he asked, which meant, *Is this man bothering you?* I started to say, "I'm fine, he's with me," but didn't get it out because I noticed an attractive woman, well behind the man, entering the real-books section of the store.

I closed my eyes, then opened them again, but it was still Lynn.

"Jesus Christ!" I said in a low voice, but loud enough that Kim heard me. "Sorry," I said to him. He nodded and moved his hand as if to say, *It's okay,* but I felt bad anyway. I still thought the man's ideas were loopy, but I could see how that might be offensive to him. But I had no time to worry about it, because Lynn was approaching our table. She walked straight to us, glaring, and more shame swelled inside me. I looked down at the old book sitting open in front of me, and froze into inaction, not knowing what to do.

"Mr. Ares?" the store manager said again, looking cross at Kim, as if he was the cause of the pale shade on my face.

"Yes, Mr. Ares," said Lynn, arriving at the spot. "That *is* you, isn't it?" She smiled at the other men, putting them further off guard. "Am I interrupting something?"

"May I help you, ma'am?" the man said to her, to which she smiled again and told him she was my wife. He looked at me, and I tried to regain my composure, my mind still scrambling.

"Yes, this is quite a surprise," I said to the men. "I appreciate your help." Then, pointing down at the open Bible, "Do you need to put this away?"

"Are you finished with it?" the man asked, and Kim got up from the table, realizing that theology class was over for today.

"No," Lynn said with another smile, moving to the seat just vacated. "I'd like to see what you've been reading."

"Very well," the man said, not sure what to make of her tone. "Let us know if you need anything else."

I was frozen into inaction, but fortunately Kim broke the ice by blurting out to Lynn that he was Presidio class of '44. She politely but distractedly acknowledged him, and the little man realized he was not welcome anymore, so he said, "I guess I'll be going, I'm hungry for some dinner. . . . Have a good one!" As he left, I felt a pang of guilt that I had revealed too much to him, but then my attention shifted back to Lynn and a much bigger pang took over. I didn't say anything, but just stared at her as she sat down across from me, resolutely pulling off her pair of long, thin gloves.

13

"How did you get here?" I asked, curious because she didn't like to travel in an aero alone. I was also trying to buy myself some time to come up with an explanation for why in the world I had been reading this book. *Anything but the truth.*

"The shuttle," she said as she finished settling into a posture that said, as clearly as it could without words, *I'm not leaving until I find out what's going on.* She continued. "I'm tired of sitting at home. I keep getting calls about the funeral, which I don't want to deal with. So I thought I'd come to the castle and join you in the investigation, then go home with you." She saw my disapproving expression, then added, "It's *my* daughter, too."

"How did you find me?" I asked.

"Security at the garage called around and told me you walked out into the city looking for a bookstore. They took me to the tunnel entrance and stayed with me until I found this one. The man at the front told me where you were." I grunted in admiration, and she added, "I guess you're not the only detective in our family."

"Well, it's good to see you, anyway," I said, hoping some charm might divert her from her task, but feeling angry inside at the intrusion. "I wasn't sure if you wanted me anymore."

"Who else do I have?" she said, then realized how it sounded, so she grabbed my hand. "What I mean is, we need to get through this together." I put my other hand on top of hers, and it felt good. For about three seconds.

"That's why I need to know what's going on," she concluded, putting the last hand on the pile and squeezing. "So, what *is* going on, Michael? I've been trying to trust you, God knows I have, but I just *know* there's something you're not telling me. And I've always been right before."

My mind raced, and I knew she would feel the sweat forming on my hands, so I withdrew them and rubbed my temples. *Anything but the truth,* I thought, because I knew for sure that I would lose her if every time she looked at me, she saw the man who had killed her daughter. I didn't know if *I* could live with myself, so how could she?

"Does it have something to do with this book?" she asked, pulling it from in front of me and swinging it around to see what it was. Then, "You've got to be kidding me."

"Saul says it's good reading, especially when you're working on a case." I had nothing better at the time. "It also talks about life after death."

"Well, that sounds good," she said, pushing the book away as if she had decided it was irrelevant. "So what's going on?"

Mixed in with the anger, guilt, and panic I was feeling, there was something else. It was almost imperceptible in the maelstrom of emotions, but I registered it nonetheless, because I had quite a bit of experience at sensing danger under duress. I held a finger up to Lynn to suspend our conversation and looked around at the people within view, cataloging them all in a matter of seconds. And that's when I realized that the man just inside the entrance to the real-books section was listening to us.

He was big, bearded, facing half away from us as he looked through a stack of books. He wore a milky-purple handkerchief tied around his head (a style only slightly out-of-date), and the black-on-black multilayered clothing that was never passé. He was much too far away to hear us naturally, but I was almost sure he was listening nonetheless. He had a nice pair of glasses hanging out of his left jacket pocket, with their lenses facing our way, but he was also wearing a pair. I surmised that the ones in his pocket were equipped with a listening device that projected a vacuum tunnel straight out from the lenses, picking up sound for up to a hundred meters in that direction and piping it to the other set of glasses. Though the man was moving back and forth naturally, checking out various bookstands around him, he kept the side of his body, and thus the hanging glasses, pointed toward us at all times. It was an old trick, though not many knew it.

The figure also seemed familiar somehow, which strengthened my suspicions, but after a few moments of careful scrutiny, I still didn't recognize him. I decided to avoid a confrontation if possible, in case it was someone from BASS, or from Saul himself. I didn't want to give any hints that I knew what was going on, until it was time for me to act.

"Let's get some fresh air," I said to Lynn, and stood up.

"Fresh air . . . in the city?" she said as she gathered her gloves and let me take her arm in my hand, escorting her out of the real-books section. Sure enough, the bandanna man moved to another shelf, giving us a wide berth as we left.

I exited the store into what was now night in the city, putting the herd of people on the sidewalk between us and the entrance. Then I headed to the corner, looking back to see if the man came out after us. When I was fairly sure he hadn't, I turned the corner and then another one, finally planting myself and Lynn apart from the street crowd in a darker, recessed entrance to a vacant building that was being retrofitted. I leaned on some posters of an upcoming holofilm, while she put her designer gloves back on.

"I'm freaking out here," she said. "I need to know what's going on, and I need to know before we go anywhere else." She looked around, presumably to make sure she really wanted to stay there for more than a few seconds. "It has to do with Lynette, right?"

Not distracted any longer, I looked at her full lips, the wind-blown hair, and the imperfections in her complexion that were still slightly visible in certain kinds of light, despite the best makeup money could buy. Deep down, pangs of conscience were nudging me to tell her the truth, hoping against hope that true love could conquer anything.

"Okay," I started. "There *is* something going on. But if I tell you, you'll wish I hadn't. That's why I'm so reticent."

She cringed for a second, then said, "Try me."

"You need to be sure about this," I added, wanting there to be no doubt that this was a full revelation. "Because it involves someone who has been very important in your life."

"Are you going to tell me you know who killed my daughter?" she said impatiently.

I exhaled, and nodded. "Yes, I know."

"What! You know! How long have you known this?" Her gloves were fists now. "Why didn't you tell me? Is he in custody . . . ?" By now I was waving my hands in front of me, to stop her tirade, but also to stop her blows if she decided to start beating on me again.

"It's not that easy, Lynn. In fact, it's very complicated." She pushed her fists down to her sides.

"Who. Killed. My. Daughter," she said through clenched teeth.

"Saul did," I said.

The color immediately and visibly drained from her face and arms. She looked at the ground, then back at me with her mouth open, like it was paralyzed. But then she started shaking her head slowly, left to right.

"No." Now looking me in the eye. "I don't believe it."

Not even any questions! Just a summary pronouncement of innocence for the old man, and guilt on me, calling me a liar. I was incredulous, and instantly angry, feeling the inert rage spark to life inside me. I was telling her the truth, in a way, but I could tell from her expression that she wasn't going to believe me, even if I could have proven it.

"What do you mean you don't believe it? I'm telling you, *Saul killed Lynette.*"

"And I can tell you're not telling me the truth, or at least the whole truth," she said, holding my gaze. "I know you too well, Michael. Besides, Saul would never do such a thing. . . ."

At that moment, we both became aware that a figure had detached itself from the flowing mob on the sidewalk and was limping toward us, obscured by the lights from the street. We knew it was a woman by the voice, jabbering as she approached. And as she entered our mild light, we saw that she was homeless, or at least close to it.

". . . Cuz I know yodo wanno *trouble.* I jez wanshowyou sumpin yodonsee muchesedays." And she promptly removed an arm and then a leg, holding them in her one good arm and still standing—an impressive feat of balance. "What ahneed, ofcose, ista get danew stuff. I know you haf sumptin—dose gluffs ah Hampwin, ain't dey?"

My rage transferring to the lady, I moved my left hand across to my right thigh, pulled up my jacket, and liberated one of the boas with my right hand. I thrust my arm straight out and pointed the imposing weapon at the beggar's face, a few inches from her nose.

"Take a walk," I said, too angry to realize what I was saying.

The woman pivoted on her one good leg and hopped off, awkwardly trying to attach her fake limbs and muttering "yes-sir" over and over again.

When she was gone, I replaced the boa and finally met Lynn's stare, which was a cross between pain and perplexity.

"What?" I said rhetorically.

She studied me like I was a gross science experiment for a moment, then shook her head.

"What makes you think Saul killed Lynnie?" she asked.

"Paul told me," I answered, and looked away because she was really making me uncomfortable. When I looked back, she was shaking her head again.

"Come on, Lynn, wake up!" It felt better to be on the offensive. "The old man is your benefactor. Of course you don't want to believe this. But I'm telling you, it's the truth. If you won't trust Paul, trust me."

"When you say Saul killed her," she asked, "you don't mean directly, do you? He's a sick old man. He doesn't do bombs . . ."

"Right," I said, scrambling to keep up with her detective skills. "He made someone else do it, of course." Immediately I regretted saying that, and became visibly panicked when she said "Who?" because I had no answer planned.

When she saw my expression and heard the deafening silence that ensued, her bearing changed for the worse over the next few moments into something I had never seen in her, at least not toward me. She actually staggered a few steps toward the street, like she might run away.

"I don't even know you." She shook her head some more,

and I met her angry stare. I knew what she was thinking, and I was powerless against it. *"You?"* Those full lips were twisted into a rectangle, framing both sets of teeth. "*You.* You killed her. *You killed my daughter?"* She was backing away more, still piercing my eyes with hers.

"Lynn, what in the world are you talking about?" But I felt like a liar, and I knew that I was looking like one to her.

"Oh my God!" The last word became a half scream, and it really looked like she was going to run. So I lunged at her and got her by the shoulders. She kicked and screamed, and I felt the pain from both.

"Okay, Lynn, the honest truth." She stopped kicking and screaming almost instantly, but looked down, her tangle of streaked hair facing me. I went on. "I'm sorry, I'm so sorry. I don't know what to do. It's the worst." She looked up at me, tears now on her cheeks, but the bitterness was still there.

"The old man is losing it. He might have been a great man once, but he's losing it. He put this . . . *thing* in my head a long time ago, so he could make me do what I didn't want to do. He used me to kill them—I didn't even know I was doing it. *He* is to blame, not me, for God's sake!"

"How did you find out about this?" she said, shrugging off my grasp.

"Paul told me. He's broken up over it, too. But we have to deal with the old man. We're the only ones who can." She wiped her face with the gloves and took a step backward again.

"Lynn, you can't say anything about this," I pleaded, sensing that she was leaving and this time I wouldn't be able to stop her. "And we can't talk about it at home. Remember how Saul wouldn't let us on our property while the house was being built? I think it has cameras, or microphones, if not some other scary modifications. I'm not sure what he was up to. . . ."

"I'll talk to him about it," she said, still backing away.

"No, Lynn, you *cannot* talk to him. He will kill me—and you, too. You have to let Paul and me deal with him. We'll prove it, and clear my name."

"Clear your name?" She grunted. "You're the one who dragged me and Lynnie into this mess . . . *clear that*!" She looked behind her, at the crowd, then looked back at me. "I'll believe you, if that's what you want, but I don't want to see you anymore. Do whatever you're gonna do, but don't come home. I won't be there anyway."

She turned and surged back out to the street and into the swarm of people. I followed her, shouting her name and that she wasn't thinking straight, but I soon lost her. She probably caught one of the numerous taxis loitering in the area, and headed out of the city to God knows where.

As I was pondering a wide range of next moves—from blowing my brains out to chasing her down—I caught the bandanna man out of the corner of my eye. His height gave him away in the crowd on the other side of the street. My attention and energy now directed at this stalker, I crossed the street, trying to keep an eye on him while avoiding the traffic. He saw me and moved away down the block, but he did so in a manner that seemed to beckon me to follow.

After following him around a corner, I saw the purple pate

disappear into the buildings halfway down the block. Upon reaching the spot, I found only a dark alley about two cars wide. I paused after only three or four initial steps into it, but already it was much quieter and darker than out on the street. There were numerous shadows on both sides of the alley, in fact, where the man or many others could have been hidden. It was a good spot for an ambush.

I slipped the glasses on, switching them to night vision, and panned the shadowy places carefully. It would have been better if the alley had been entirely dark, because the contrasts caused by the minimal light still left some possible hiding places unexposed.

I pulled out the stopper boa and held it ready as I advanced farther into the darkness.

14

"Michael," said a voice from the shadows. I spun instinc-tively toward it, but then wasn't sure of the direction, because it had echoed throughout the alley. "It's me. Paul."

I had realized it was his voice a second before he said that, and from these new words I located the shadows where he stood in time to see him step out of them. I didn't lift the gun but still held it ready, feeling a streak of suspicion.

"Sorry about the cloak-and-dagger," he said. *And beard-and-bandanna,* I thought as I admired his disguise in the half-light. I remembered that he had several such getups for occasional forays into the city—he was simply too recognizable to venture out as himself. "I had to talk to you about our . . . problem," he continued, "and there was no way I could do it safely in the castle. When I heard that you walked off, I thought this was a perfect opportunity. But by the time I found you, Lynn was there."

"And you didn't know if I had told her," I said, returning the gun to its holster. "So you were listening to us."

"I *thought* that was why you noticed me," he said with a relieved smile. "I was worried that you might have actually recognized me, and I'd have to scrap this look."

"No, it's quite good really," I said, stepping a little closer and testing it further. It was amazing how different someone could look with just a few simple additions. "But now that I know it's you . . ." A BASS siren screamed by out on the street, distracting us both for a moment. Then I said, "What's happening?"

"Too much, too fast," he said. "You won't believe the timing, but I found out when Min is going in for maintenance."

"Oh?" I said, switching off the glasses' night vision and taking them off, but not before noticing in them that it was 8:22 P.M.

"Tonight, at three or four A.M.—we have to find out which."

"Tonight?" I said, struck by the suddenness, my mind convulsing with the implications. "You're kidding me."

"No. This is it." Paul's eyes narrowed as he nodded, anticipating a grim satisfaction. "Tonight we will avenge D and your daughter." I wondered again what this meant to him—would he want to put away his own father, or did he have something else in mind? I wasn't able to ask him yet, because he continued. "But before that, we have work to do. I have a ground car on the street. Come with me."

He didn't speak as we made our way through the streams of people to the car, probably because he didn't trust his disguise implicitly, or he was worried about my being recognized. But once we were sitting in the car with the doors safely closed, he turned his attention back to me.

"The tech is a problem," he said, and at first I didn't know what he was referring to, but then my conversation with Kim in the bookstore reemerged into my mind after being buried by the talk with Lynn and the encounter with Paul. "He's very good at what he does, and if he decides to start snooping around the company for ROM 717, he may find out more than we want him to know . . . more than *you* want him to know. He may discover that you're the murderer, and who knows what he'll do with that. Or his snooping may be detected by the old man and ruin our chance to confront him tonight."

I realized as Paul said this that he must have been watching and listening to me in the store long before I had noticed him. He knew what I had said to Kim, and had probably been worried about it right away, but couldn't have done anything about it then because Lynn had shown up, and he'd wanted to see what that was all about.

"You told me the black op was called Mind Lift," I said. "But now I hear it's ROM 717. What's up with that?"

"The old man changed the name along the way," Paul answered. "He's been going off the deep end into some scary religious stuff. But we need to deal with the tech, right now."

"What do you suggest?" I said, feeling the aggression rising within me again, as if my subconscious knew where this was going before I admitted it to my conscious mind. When those thoughts started rolling in, I felt shame and tried to think of other options, but to no avail. “I don’t think Kim can be bought, judging from what I know of him.” I was thinking of the man’s spiritual slant, of course, and then another option did occur to me. “He has a strong moral sense . . . maybe we could confide in him to some degree, and he could help us once he knows what’s wrong with Saul . . . ?”

“Maybe,” Paul said unconvincingly, “but if something happens tonight, I’ll have a much easier time tying up any loose ends if no one else knows what we know.” There was that hint of homicide again, for the old man and for Kim, which simultaneously made my blood boil more and brought back the flash of shame. It also felt so awkward and unnatural to be talking about covering up a crime when I had spent the last eight years of my life trying to uncover them.

“Either way,” Paul continued, “we have to do something about it. Call the tech and find out where he is. He said he was going to get something to eat.” Paul had heard that, too, and remembered it, which was more than I could say.

I fumbled for the glasses in my pocket and dialed Kim, confused about what to do and therefore retreating to the ease and safety of just doing what my friend and boss had said. The Korean man answered and said he was a few blocks away, finishing his food, and promised to wait for me there when I told him I wanted to talk with him again. I didn’t mention Paul, thinking that might spook him.

After I told Paul where the tech was, the younger Rabin turned on the car and put on his glasses, tapping them a few times and telling them to start a running trace on any Net activity by Kim, "just in case he gets curious before we get there." And then, no sooner than he had pulled out into the slow-moving, stop-and-start traffic on the street, he said, "No way!" and informed me that Kim had already begun searching the Net and the BASS database for ROM 717.

"Wow," I responded. "He'll find it, right? Because he's good."

"He may be good," Paul answered, "but I have the master keys." He moved his finger on the arm of the glasses and recited some codes and commands into them, which I didn't understand, but I knew he was somehow limiting the tech's access to BASS data, effectively blocking the search. "There's no way he'll cut through that ice before we get there." He took his glasses off and surveyed the traffic ahead, sighing. "*If* we ever get there."

We sat in silence for a few moments as he navigated along one of San Francisco's trademark streets, narrow and sharply inclined. One of the old cable-car trolleys, still used throughout the city as a reminder of its past and as an attraction for tourists, it added to the congestion until Paul could maneuver around it.

"*Did* you tell Lynn?" he then asked me. I hesitated for a moment, not understanding why my trust in him was no longer absolute but wondering if it had something to do with how he had trailed me—an experience I wasn't used to having with friends.

"Yes," I said, putting aside the feeling. "I pleaded with her not to talk to the old man, but I felt like I had to tell her."

"I understand," he said sympathetically, rewarding my

trust and allaying my suspicions. "But this is all the more reason why we have to move soon."

"Is there some other reason?" I asked, sensing that there was.

Now it was his turn to pause. Perhaps he was deciding how much he should trust *me.*

"The longer we go," he finally said, "the more chance the old man will find out that you know, or find out that I'm . . ." *betraying him* seemed to fit, but he said, "not approving of what he's doing." Almost unconsciously, he touched a few buttons on the dash, making sure that his privacy system was on and working. "I'm just afraid he might make a move himself—if he suspects anything—like trip the hardware in your head."

"And kill me?" I said, still mystified that all this was happening. He looked at me and nodded, then knitted his brows in thought as he turned back to the street.

"He asked me to bring you to a meeting tonight, at ten o'clock, in the Parthenon Room. It's more than a little strange; I'm not sure what to make of it."

"What kind of meeting?" I asked.

"A summit," he answered, and I thought that it was strange indeed, because I had never previously been invited to one. I knew what they were, though: a group of "powerful friends" (which was a considerable understatement) came to the castle to ingratiate themselves with the old man, hear about his latest achievements in technology, and perhaps wrangle about their sale and use—which, up until now, the Mayor had guarded penuriously. This frustrated the moguls to no end, but effectively elevated BASS and its leader to an ever-increasing position of power among them.

"He invited me just today? Or before today?" I asked.

"No one is invited before today," he said. "That's how the summits work. *Day of* . . . for security purposes. Any advance planning would be too noticeable by people who might be fishing the net for something like this. A revealing data pattern might become visible for a split second, and before you know it, an interested party could disrupt the entire global economy by taking out a whole handful of world leaders with one well-placed nuke. Even *day of* has its risks, but it's unlikely anyone can put together a serious threat that quickly."

And they had to talk face-to-face, I knew, from when I had asked the old man about these meetings in the past. Any discussions over the net were too vulnerable to data thieves, and, as Saul had said with his tired smile, "It still all comes down to real men." I took this to have a double meaning: real as opposed to virtual, and those who could get it done as opposed to those who couldn't.

"So . . . what about this is worrying you?" I asked, wanting to know if I should be worried.

"I don't know for sure," he said, appearing again like he was trying to decide how much to say. "Something has occurred to me, but it's farfetched." I looked at him and raised my eyebrows, indicating that I wanted to hear it.

"Well," Paul continued, "what if he does know something, and he's setting you up? Maybe he wants to make you look bad, or he's hoping you'll lose it in front of these people. Or maybe he'll *make* you do something stupid, with the chip." He shook his head. "I don't know. It's just that your reputation isn't spotless right now with that clip that was sent all over the net. You discredited Harris, but somehow stains like that linger in the public consciousness, even against all good sense."

"You're saying that the old man leaked that tape," I said, "because he plans to kill me like D, and somehow that will prevent suspicion."

"I'm not saying that," Paul answered as he watched the crowd file by at an intersection. "It's just a fear. But either way, we need to move. Tonight. With the way our Sabon technology is progressing, the old man is on the verge of becoming one of the most powerful men in the world, if not *the* most powerful—and we can't let that happen." He gave me a purposeful look. "We can't let a psychopath shape our future. Too many people would be hurt."

The anger in me had diverted from Lynn or Kim or anyone else and was now focused completely on Saul. I visualized killing him tonight, in his top-floor crypt, and I studied the eyes of my friend, which sparkled between the beard and bandanna.

"What do you want to do?" I asked.

"We go to Cyber Hole after we deal with Kim," he answered, and I noticed that we were approaching the restaurant. "We find out exactly when Min will be there, and how long. Then we go to the summit, and pretend nothing's wrong." He looked at me, as if to see whether I was capable of that. "Then, when Min is gone, I'll tell the old man that he needs to invite you up to his floor, right away, for a talk. He'll do it."

There was a long silence, until I realized he wasn't going to continue, and it was up to me to raise the question.

"And then what?" I said finally.

"Then I would say it's up to you," he answered. "It was your daughter, after all. You can shoot the old man—we'll put a gun in his hand, and I'll say it was self-defense. Or you can try to get a confession out of him, and if you can, we'll have him locked up." I felt some surprise at his first option, even given the circumstances, but I asked about the second.

"How would we get a confession?"

"The original camera system is still there, in the penthouse, but it's turned off. The entrance scan clears you from recording equipment, so he'll feel safe to speak freely, and he might, if we confront him together. Before we do, I'll simply turn on the system from his security room—I know how to do it. Whatever he says will be recorded."

Just then we arrived in front of the restaurant, and seeing that there were no legal parking spaces open (of course), Paul pulled into a loading zone.

"I know what you're thinking," he said as he activated the external windshield display that allowed him to park anywhere. "But I'm actually much closer to you than I am to him. And as I said, he's lost it, and he has to pay the price. One way or the other." I thought I saw his jaw harden, but wasn't sure because of the beard. "So it's up to you, Michael."

He switched the engine off, and looked at me as if he was waiting for an answer.

"Turn the cameras on," I said, "and we'll see what happens."

15

"This is the place, right?" Paul asked, looking through the windshield at the storefront on the right ahead of us. "Ridley's Deli?"

"Yeah," I answered, then noticed through the crowd on the sidewalk that Kim was standing just outside the restaurant, to the right of it, wearing his cyber rig and looking obviously nervous, his eyes panning from our car to the crowd and back again. "He's out there waiting for us," I told Paul, who grunted and stepped out of the car. I did the same on my side and we both took a few steps toward Kim.

When he saw us come out of the car, the little Korean blurred into motion and took off with abandon through the crowd and down the sidewalk, away from us, creating a ripple effect in the pedestrians and eliciting surprised shouts from them as he jostled them on his way.

"Why's he running?" I said, as Paul and I looked at each other.

"I don't know," the big man said. "But we can't lose him." He thought for a second, then raised his eyebrows and nodded. He said, "Come 'ere," and moved to the back of his car with the excitement of a young boy who finally gets to play with a favorite toy. And that was exactly what he was about to do, as it turned out. He spoke a voice command that sounded like "wintermute"—or maybe it was "interview"—I couldn't be sure in the din of the street. But the trunk slid open and he was soon holding two cylindrical objects, one in each hand, that looked something like the handle grips on a bicycle or motorcycle, with slight depressions for each finger. He took a step back from the open trunk, held them in front of him just like he was riding a bike, and moved his wrists backward like he was revving a motorcycle. Two dark shapes rose from the trunk, sprouted wings, and hovered above the car.

"I haven't practiced so much to never use them," he said. After manipulating something on the remote-control stick in his right hand, he handed it to me and said, "Take a moment to get the feel while I start after him. It's intuitive." He grabbed his glasses with his now empty right hand, slid them on, and headed after the fleeing Kim on foot, the falcon speeding ahead of him above the traffic and the crowd. I put mine on then and immediately saw a flashing notice of a wireless interface beckoning me. I selected it and the hovering bird's view filled my eyes.

"Tap your index finger to take it out of standby." Paul's voice said in my glasses. He was already puffing with exertion. I did as he had said, and the falcon immediately started to drop until I jerked the remote back up. "Your index finger is a mouse to select view and other options, middle finger squeeze twice to fire stopper rounds, ring finger for killers, and your pinkie for gas." I moved my wrist forward and backward, like a motorcycle grip, and watched the falcon dive and ascend, then tilted my hands sideways each way for it to turn, then figured out for myself that the thumb controlled acceleration and reverse.

I sailed the bird in different directions above the street, then pointed it toward an empty section of wall high up on a building, depressed my pinkie twice, and watched a gas pellet streak to the wall and explode against it. Satisfied that I basically knew what I was doing, I minimized the falcon's view in my glasses by half, so that I could see in front of me, and immediately noticed that the crowd had parted from me in all directions, forming a circle from which they stared at me in shocked silence like I was some kind of alien invader. Taking this as my cue to move, I jogged off in the direction my two coworkers had gone, keeping my wrist and fingers stationary and pressing my thumb against the throttle so that the falcon stayed right above me.

As I progressed toward the corner that Kim and Paul had disappeared around, I practiced watching the street through the clear portion of the glasses and the falcon's view through the rest. The former was harder than the latter: I didn't have to worry much about the falcon as long as my hand was in the same position, because unless a BASS aero showed up at some point, there was nothing at that height that the bird could run into. Some of the ad holos were projected up there, and I couldn't see much when the falcon was inside them, but I knew that if I just held steady, I could fly straight through them and out the other side.

When I reached the next block, Paul told me which way he had gone and sent me in the other direction. I combed that length of street for Kim, sending the falcon ahead to look around the corners at the next intersection.

"This would be a lot easier with the Eye," I said.

"Which we can't use, of course," Paul replied. "Because it could be detected."

"What if Saul already knows what we're doing?"

"I don't think it's likely with the blocks I'm using," he said. "They'll keep Kim from diving too deep and keep us hidden at the same time. Hold on." I kept combing my street and waited until he came back on. "According to the trace, he's diving right now, so look for someone standing still. I don't think he can move when he's in."

"Right," I said, remembering how the tech had gone rigid in the net room at the castle. "Can you tell what he's doing? Calling for help?"

"He's all over the place," Paul said. "Trying avenues other than BASS, so that proves he found out something about the murder, and he thinks I'm in league with you . . . two big shots, so he's not expecting any help from the company. He also probably won't go in the stores, because he's figured out by now that my junk may be good enough to access their security systems." As he paused, I studied all the stationary figures on two streets, and then a third as I turned the falcon around and sent it around another corner. Then Paul added, "But he's straining my ice, so we need to find him fast."

As if on cue, through the falcon's view, I noticed a familiar male form flush against a pole. I zoomed closer and saw that it was indeed Kim.

"I've got him," I said.

"I know," Paul answered, and, guessing my question, added, "I'm plugged in to your glasses and falcon view, too. Only because I've practiced . . . I wouldn't try that many perspectives if I were you. What street is he on? Either find a street sign or bring up the GPS." Not wanting to take my eyes off Kim, I moved my pointer finger until the falcon's location was at the top right of its screen, and told Paul where it was.

"I'm northwest on Mason," he said. "My bird can be there in a minute, me in five."

"We need to take him out now, while he's under," I said, then paused for a moment, realizing I was in a kill mode by default from the adrenaline and anger inside me, but wondering if I should be.

"Suit yourself," Paul said.

"If I gas him or use stoppers," I said, my mind firing in all directions, "what would we do with him?"

"Lock him up somewhere, I suppose," Paul said through heavy breaths, obviously running in my direction. "I just don't see how that's going to work with what we have to do tonight." He then added, "Don't use gas . . . BASS sensors might pick it up."

I tried to think harder, which didn't work too well, but

then my reverie was broken as Kim came out of his dive and saw the menacing black bird floating near him. He instinctively leaped in the direction his body was facing and raced into the tangle of slow-moving cars on the street. I jerked the falcon forward in the direction of his receding back, and when I had closed the distance to a couple of car lengths, I tried to put the crosshairs on his zigzagging form as best I could, squeezed my second finger twice, then held it down. I was expecting to see a stream of X-shaped projectiles raining down on the man, but instead I could tell right away that they were regular bullets slamming into the cars and road surface all around him. When I realized this, I abruptly stopped firing and braked the bird, watching Kim continue through the gauntlet of cars and then people on the sidewalk on the other side of the street. I was amazed that he hadn't been killed, and wondered if he had been wounded. Either way, I knew he wouldn't stop running from us now.

"You said the middle finger was stoppers!" I yelled to Paul.

"No, I didn't," he yelled back. "I said the middle finger was killers . . . think about it, Michael, it makes sense." He chuckled. "Look at the control menu if you don't believe me. . . . Are you okay, man? Is the stress getting to you?"

Regardless of who was right about what had been said, the stress definitely was getting to me, to one degree or another. I realized that I had been leaning against an occupied car when the driver suddenly laid on his horn, startling me out of my reverie. After moving away from it, I said to Paul, "You tell me what to do."

"Just keep him from doubling back," my friend said. "I'm heading him off."

I moved the falcon forward until I caught sight of Kim again, and then had to will my body to start moving forward itself, because it was much more natural to stand still when manipulating the flying machine and looking through its eyes.

"He's turning west on Sutter," I told Paul a minute later.

"Perfect. I'm almost at the other end of the block."

Both of our falcons turned their respective corners at about the same time, and then we ourselves arrived on each end of the street a little while later. When we did, I saw through my human eyes both falcons hovering in the air in the middle of the block, turning in every direction, seeking Kim from their bird's-eye view. I couldn't see Paul on the other end of the block because of the people, cars, trolleys, and ad holos, but I knew he was scanning his end of the street, like I was mine. None of this yielded any sign of Kim, however, even after a few minutes of searching.

"Did he get past you?" I asked.

"No way."

"The subway?"

No answer initially . . . Paul was probably studying a map in his glasses. Then: "Nope. The nearest entrance is just beyond my position."

"Bloody hell," I said. "Where is he? He must have gone into a building."

More pregnant silence as Paul's monster software checked all the businesses on the block. "Not that I can see."

"Is he diving right now?"

"I don't think so."

I moved against the corner of the corner building, filled the glasses with the falcon's view, and scanned the street again as thoroughly as I could, keeping some distance from Paul's bird so that we didn't overlap too much. After a few more minutes of this, I gave up and minimized the falcon's view again, only to be startled again by Paul, who was now standing right in front of me.

"Let's check back this way," he said, gesturing behind me with his head.

"You think he got past me?" I asked.

"Well, you're not exactly in tiptop shape, buddy." He patted me on the shoulder. "You go this way and I'll go that way, okay?"

"Okay," I said, and he left, his falcon streaking through the air from the middle of the block and around the corner to the street he had entered. I stood in place for a few moments, staring back down the street we had been searching, a feeling of defeat now added to my anger. My falcon hovered between the high buildings, and the crowd seemed to have thinned out a bit . . . perhaps some people had been creeped out by the black birds and migrated away or into the stores along the street.

Thinking about the stores drew my attention to the ad holos, which I usually ignored because they were so ubiquitous in the city. But something splintered in the back of my mind, so I studied the fanciest one in my vicinity, which was on the other side of the street and a short distance up the block. It was a big one protruding from the second story of a building, above the entrance to a travel agency, and it alternated between a seascape with a water-ski boat spraying virtual water onto the sidewalk, tuxedos crowded around a spinning roulette wheel in Monte Carlo, and a dusty high-powered jeep filled with adventurers on safari in Nevada. The genetically engineered lions they were hunting leaped down dramatically to the edge of the street, then disappeared. After a few moments, the sequence repeated itself.

Next I looked on my side of the street at a seven-foot-tall hologram filling the air above an ad projector in the sidewalk, displaying real estate that was available for purchase or rental throughout the city. I moved out to the curb and farther so I could get a more unobstructed view of the holo, and saw that it was currently advertising a town home, presenting it in a life-like yet shrunken three-dimensional reproduction. While I was staring at it, the image dissolved into another three-story for sale, and as it did, I might have seen the shape of a human figure inside the big ad, but thought that it was likely just my imagination. The holo did seem to be slightly distorted, however, so I glanced at the other big one across the street again for comparison.

Then I noticed a similar real estate ad farther down the block on that side, so I brought the falcon down next to it to see if it looked any different from the one closer to me. I couldn't tell in the falcon's camera, which was one step away from reality, so I walked toward the holo house near me and brought the falcon toward it from the other side. As I and the bird closed in on the big ad, people gave us a wide birth and watched from a distance. Soon the only objects on that stretch of sidewalk were me, the virtual building, and the falcon floating on the other side of it. I looked at it through my glasses and through the falcon's view, but couldn't tell for sure if it looked any different from the other. So I slowly stepped toward the holo and stretched my hand out. I moved my body forward gradually, and my hand and arm started disappearing into the ad. . . .

Kim exploded into me out of the holo with both arms extended, sending me sprawling to the sidewalk, and ran off in the direction I had come from. I instinctively rolled sideways and came off my back into a crouched position facing that direction, my knuckles resting on the cement. But before I could spring up to pursue him, a violent crash behind me ripped my eardrums and pelted me with hot gas and shards of metal, sending me sprawling again, this time onto my stomach. I looked back to see the glowing, smoking remains of the falcon, then realized what had happened. Being inexperienced with the remote, I had held on to it too long, first sending the bird upward with wrists flayed back to stop my fall, then bringing it crashing down when I rolled and pointed my hands down on the pavement. If I had just let go of the stick, presumably the bird would have been fine.

Now even more pissed and homicidal, I yanked out the killer boa and surged around the corner to pursue Kim.

"Paul, I found him, he's on . . ." I looked around for a street sign and had to crane my neck because the blank black window for the falcon was still showing in the right side of my glasses. I turned it off and could see much better, but then realized there were three ways the tech could have run from here, and I didn't know where he was. "I lost my falcon. Paul, he's somewhere near Bush and Taylor." A few moments passed. "Paul?"

I continued running straight up Taylor, because that was the most direct route away from where I was, and after a block or so, I thought I heard some screams ahead and to the left. "Paul," I said again.

"Yeah, buddy," he finally said. "I'm on California, but don't come over here. Nobody knows who I am because of this getup, but someone will recognize you. I'm leaving the falcon for right now to keep the gawkers at bay. Catch me on Taylor, on the way back to the car."

I slowed to a jog but kept moving up the street, now hearing Paul's voice modified through the falcon's megaphone, a way that we often cleared a crime scene. Almost immediately I saw him turn the corner, briskly moving toward me. He grabbed my arm and spun me around in the other direction, back to where we had come from.

"What the hell happened?" I asked.

"You won't believe it," he said. "This is worse than I thought, and you don't want to see the results."

Now I grabbed his arm and pulled him to a stop. I said, "I do," and wrenched the falcon's remote out of his hand.

"Okay, hold on," he said, and synced his bird to my glasses.

I felt the now-familiar rush of vertigo when the falcon's view filled mine, and heard its looped announcement telling people to move on, stay back, etc. With the remote, I pulled the bird out of its autopiloted orbit and took it toward what it was circling, which turned out to be a macabre scene, to say the least. One of the retro trolleys was stopped on an empty patch of street, and next to the tracks behind it was the bottom half of Kim's body. It took me only a moment to figure out that the top half was underneath the cable car.

"What the . . . ?"

"That's what I was trying to tell you," Paul said, grabbing the remote back and moving me along again down the street. I was too dumbfounded to resist. "I found the tech with the falcon and was coming close to him, and all of a sudden he seizes up like when he's diving the net, and like a zombie he throws himself under the front wheels of the trolley."

"You're kidding me."

"He might have just tried to make one last dangerous dive to escape, maybe tried to hack the falcon or something, and lost control of himself . . . but I think it was the old man, taking control of him." Paul pointed to his head, and, as if by reflex, he looked all around and quickened his pace. "The tech's persistent attempts at searching for the black-ops project probably triggered something that the old man noticed. He didn't want us to find out whatever Kim knew, so he tried to help him escape, maybe. But then when we were closing in, he definitely had to do something."

He stopped, took hold of my shoulders, and looked at me in earnest.

"Listen, Michael. We *cannot* use the net anymore tonight. Do you understand?"

"I don't bloody understand much of anything right now, Paul."

"Do you understand?"

"Yes."

"Good." He started walking fast again.

"What will you do about Kim?" I said, feeling shame again for using the man's name.

"It's a suicide," he answered. "I'll just file the report."

"But what if some peacers start looking into it?"

"They won't," he said confidently. "I have the master keys, remember?"

"I'm feeling something in my head here," I said, pointing to the general area. "Is that where the chip would be?"

"It depends on what kind of wetware it is," he said, panting again from the brisk walk. "If it's specialized to take over your will, that would be the frontal lobe in the neocortex, because that's the mission-control center of the brain. Pain or discomfort might manifest from there in the spot you're talking about. But if it is a more global application, it would be in the corpus callosum, because that's the neural bridge that ties the different parts together. It borders the occipital lobe for visuals, the temporal lobe for sound, and the parietal lobe for touch sensations. The cyber-pleasure industry does implants for the parietal lobe." He smiled briefly. "But I digress . . . If your chip is global, it's in the callosum, and that would be right where you were pointing."

As he said this, the pressure seemed to increase in that part of my head.

"Or it might just be your imagination," he said, smiling again.

"I wish."

By the time we reached the car, the falcon had caught up to us. It retracted its wings and lowered itself into its resting place in the trunk, and we drove off to Chinatown Underground to find out about our window of opportunity to confront the old man without his lethal cyborg bodyguard present. I only hoped that by then, my mind would still be my own.

16

Before long, we reached the edge of the most colorful part of the city, where the rebuilt stores and restaurants of Chinatown glowed with overcrowded neon above the cramped streets. Paul pulled the car into the entrance to the Underground's parking structure, and the elevator began descending the levels to the one he wanted.

As soon as we left the car and stepped into the dim light of the garage, we were greeted by four armed guards and a beautiful Chinese woman, dressed like an executive. I instinctively raised my hands away from the boas—especially when I noticed that all the guards' assault weapons were pointed at my midsection. I took this to mean that Paul wasn't armed.

"Could we please see your clearance for those weapons," the woman said to me, with only a small trace of an accent. I slowly reached for my card and handed it to her. After she slipped it into a handheld slot and suppressed her surprise at who I was, she gave it back. Then she handed me a silver grip, which I clasped briefly and returned to her. ID equipment like that prevented old tricks like severed fingers and skin grafts. She looked relieved after she read its display.

"We apologize for any inconvenience, Mr. Ares." The guards lowered their weapons and they all retreated to an armored van parked nearby. Paul and I walked across the garage to a door, which slid open upon the wonder that was Chinatown Underground. The garage entrances, like the pedestrian ones accessed from the storefronts on the surface, had been cleverly positioned by the architects to impress the visitor with an immediate sense of awe at the scale of the massive subterranean town.

Inside the door was a suspended walkway running left and right, narrow enough that you could see most of the Underground from any spot on it. Paul didn't linger at the immediate view but proceeded to the right along the walkway. I followed him, and we continued to stare at the scene on our left as we traversed it.

In the center of the complex was a huge open space, stretching down to the bottom and up to the ceiling, twenty stories of underground atmosphere. I could see some birds circling in the middle of it—either real ones or some clever invention of the Chinese techs. I knew it wasn't Sabon technology, because they didn't have it yet, thanks to the old man's stinginess. I swerved closer to the short wall on my left and looked down, and was rewarded with a dizzying glimpse of trees and grass at the bottom of the open space, far below the circling birds. The park was only thirteen levels down, because we were on the seventh, but I was surprised at how far away it seemed.

On each side of the wide space were protruding concourses lined with shops and speckled with consumers. And on the far side from us, barely visible because of the distance and the haze from the atmosphere, was another series of walkways like the one we were on, providing access to and from the other parking garage. It occurred to me that most of the people in the mall must have walked in from the surface, however, because our walkway and the others I saw were sparsely populated.

The narrow walk dumped us out onto the broad concourse on this side of the level, and I continued following Paul as he moved purposefully toward our destination. The concourse was filled with various establishments, the temporary ones planted in its middle and the bigger, permanent ones along the outside edge. I couldn't read Chinese, and there were no signs in English, but I knew what the attractions were. Besides the usual restaurants and stores, there were numerous cyberware shops, where a trusting Chinese or a daring American could get anything from a relaxation implant to a birth-control device called a "switch," which enabled its owner to allow or prevent conception at will by way of a neural interface.

I didn't need to be able to read the signs in order to identify the many virtual- and real-sex shops, either. China had experienced their sexual revolution late, like their technological one, but when it had finally arrived, it had done so with enough force to be referred to as the "Big Bang." Just as the absence of a Judeo-Christian ethical hangover had given them a leg up on the competition in the cyber wars, so their lack of inhibitions had led them to pioneer a new form of the oldest profession, which had now become one of the Underground's biggest commodities.

Behind many of these storefronts, some of which I was passing on my way, there were hundreds, maybe thousands of men and women (and perhaps some children) who were paid to give up their bodies while their minds were elsewhere in cyberspace. I remembered someone's explanation of the popularity of this almost necrophilic version of prostitution: the customers are torn between needing someone and wanting to be alone at the same time, which has always been the name of that particular game.

I glanced at Paul to see if he noticed these places, but he was consumed with looking for a certain storefront. I didn't like some of the feelings bubbling up within me, which probably arose from the fact that I might never see my wife again, so I turned my attention to the people we were passing. And I noticed immediately how "cyberized" this culture was, reflected even in the fashions worn by a majority of the denizens, especially their youth. Hoods, hats, and headbands equipped with trodes and jacks were everywhere, allowing the wearers to have one foot in the real world and the other in a virtual one. I imagined that they were viewing music, talking with friends across town, or even experiencing pornography as they shopped or loitered in the mall. And I thought of the frightening potential of mind control for these masses, now that I knew the technology had passed the threshold of mere communication and entertainment.

Abruptly, Paul sat down on an empty bench and patted the spot beside him. When I took it, he put his arm around me and leaned over to my ear like a lover.

"You need to go in, because I don't want to have to retire this disguise," he said, then looked at one of the storefronts, which was walled in and much more plain than the rest. He leaned back over.

"Tell them you want to know how long of a window we have to cover, for security purposes."

"Okay," I said, and stood up and walked to the door in the center of the storefront, which displayed a small group of Chinese letters. Though I can't read Chinese, I knew they translated to "Cyber Hole," because that was the name of this mecca of wetware, the unlikely corporate home for a group of Chinese supertechs who could have played the Silicon Valley like a harp, had they had any such inclination.

The door was open, so I tugged on it and walked in. Ahead of me was a brown hallway that did indeed look like a horizontal hole in the ground. I walked forward in the hall, which was empty except for the small piece of scanning equipment that followed me silently along its track in the ceiling. I recognized it as one made by BASS, too expensive to be afforded by most small countries, or any corporation with fewer than a hundred thousand employees. Cyber Hole had only eight, so that meant we were very appreciative of the fine work they had done on Min.

I assumed the little machine had identified me, since I wasn't cut to ribbons by lasers, so I opened the door at the other end of the hall and stepped into the next room. It was empty except for a few used beer cans, a cardboard box, and a pair of sneakers. The walls were also bare, except for some little black squares of holo equipment and a dried brown splash that I guessed had come from one of the beer cans.

The door on the other side of the room opened with a jerk, and a nervous tech in a yellow smock stumbled in.

"Mistah Ahhris," he said, rubbing his hands together and blinking. Then he said something in Chinese that from his expression I guessed meant "sorry." He giggled anxiously, then shrugged and pointed to himself. "English, no." He smiled at me apologetically.

"You can speak Chinese," I said, pulling out the glasses and pointing to them. As I began to put them on, the poor fellow suddenly realized that we were standing in a blank room. He let out a yelp and backed through the door, bowing repeatedly. Through the still-open door, I heard him barking at someone, and a few moments later I was standing in the observation room at the top of the Statue of Liberty, looking out upon New York Harbor through the slats in her crown. It was a nice holo, but the effect was ruined by the door, which was still half open. The tech appeared in it soon, only to yelp, retreat, and bark at someone again. Soon the room changed into a polished corporate lobby, and the tech appeared one more time, his face bright red. He started talking again, in Chinese, and I flipped through the glasses' menus until I found the translation program.

". . . You not expecting!" Laughing again. His lips were moving one way, but I heard something different through the glasses, like one of those dubbed foreign holos. "Our English man is here only in day. No night horns atlas." The translation program was obviously going to have some trouble with his dialect.

"Can you understand me?" I asked, slowly and clearly. He nodded.

"Yes, but tiny." *A little*—I got the gist.

"Good," I said. "What I want is very simple."

"Yes, yes," he said through the translator. "I am very sexually aroused." He was smiling, and I smiled, too. He must have said a word that meant "very excited."

"Mr. Rabin's bodyguard, Min, is coming here tonight."

"Yes, yes," he said. "He no home young. He is our best . . . produce."

"What *time* is he coming?" I pointed to my wrist, though my only "watch" was in my glasses.

"Yes, yes." He nodded, then looked puzzled. "Why is you ask this?" I was caught off guard for a second, but then I remembered what Paul had said. So I told him about the "security window." He made clucking noises that seemed to convey understanding.

"Four hour, in the morning," he said, holding up four fingers.

"And when will he be done?" I asked. *"Finished?"*

"Difficult to say." *That was a good translation,* I thought. "He will urinate easily or he will require adjustments." *That wasn't,* I thought, but then I figured it out. In the etymology of the dialect, that concept must have developed into the terminology for "checking out okay" or requiring no treatment. The tech continued, but I stopped him.

"When would be the *earliest* that he would leave here?" I asked, then realized that this was probably not the best thing to ask, in case the man was suspicious of me. He didn't seem to notice, however, or maybe he didn't understand. So I asked if Min would be done before the sun rose, at about 6:00 A.M. He said no.

"Thank you very much," I said, and shook his hand.

"Yes, yes," he said, smiling again. And then, as I turned to walk back through the door, he bade me well by saying, "May you grow obese on your rice!" As I walked back through the brown hallway, I took the glasses off.

Very fat, I thought with a another smile of my own, and I exited the Cyber Hole.

I sat back down next to Paul and his bandanna, leaned into his ear, and told him, "Four to six, at least."

He told me that this would be the last time we could talk about this, that I should find my way back to the castle on my own, that I should show up at the summit later on, stay cool, then wait in my office for a call sometime after 4:00 A.M.

"Get some sleep, if you can," he said as he walked away from me. "You don't look too good." I waved at him, and realized that I didn't feel too well, either. I added up the hours I had slept in the last two nights, and I could count them on one hand. But I noticed on a nearby clock (the only readable thing around) that it was only an hour before I needed to be at the summit.

I headed to the surface to catch a taxi, and only stumbled twice on the way. The escalators were moving a little too fast for me.

17

Saul Rabin was driving the taxi and Lynette was being led along the sidewalk beside me by her mother—until I realized what was happening.

My body had relaxed just enough, after taking a seat in the back of the cab, to spiral into a somnambulant, mildly hallucinatory state. I had experienced similar trips, induced by fatigue and stress, after long stints of training in the insertion coffin during the Taiwan crisis. I had never thought it would happen to me again—but even though this was a different kind of war, it was a war nonetheless.

In an attempt to keep myself awake and alert, I put on the glasses and called Lynn at home, on her cell, and in her car. All of them gave me a recorded message, so I left my own on each one, asking her to please call me and give us a chance to work this out together. As I did this, I had a horrible feeling, as real as a blow to the face, that I would never see her again. The feeling sent my adrenaline coursing again, and revived my anger at the old man. But I remembered Paul's warning about the summit, and how I could ruin our chance to confront him if I didn't control myself during the meeting.

I slipped into the dream state once more before the taxi arrived at the castle and jarred me back to reality. In the dream, I was in the big meeting room where the important people were coming to meet with the Mayor. We were all standing around in formal wear, sipping drinks and eating hors d'oeuvres, and I was scanning the crowd, trying to recognize somebody. One minute I was in my right mind, and the next I was walking like a robot to a fake plant, where I found a hidden disk bomb, like the one I had used twice in the last three days.

You must also destroy the chip in your head, the old man's crackling voice said inside my brain, so I armed the disk, stuffed it inside my mouth, and walked toward the center of the room. . . .

Before I could experience my own atomization, the scene shifted to D's house on the night of the murder.

I had just finished looking over the smoldering wreckage of the car, smelling the unmistakable aroma of what was left of its occupants, and already I wished from the bottom of my soul that I could undo what I had just done. I stared down at the right hand, which had thrown the bomb, opening and closing it repeatedly while I prayed for a pill that would make me forget. Half conscious, I felt my mind trying to make the drug appear in the dream, but my hand remained empty until I awoke.

• • •

I reached the plush waiting room, high up in the castle, a few minutes before ten, and splashed some cold water on my face in its bathroom. When I came out, Paul was in the room, greeting me with a look that contained a mixture of sympathy and warning. He had traded his black-on-black, beard, and bandanna for an inauspicious blue business suit.

"You'll have to leave the boas here, of course," he said as a small storage compartment slid out from the wall in response to his touch. "And your glasses."

I reluctantly removed my jacket and the gun belt, placing them in the drawer and watching it disappear when Paul touched it again. I felt naked, and realized then that I was definitely not dressed appropriately for the most significant meeting that I had ever attended.

"Don't worry about your clothes," Paul said, sensing my discomfort. "They'll assume you intended to dress that way. They all have their own style, and they don't follow any rules."

I suppose that's what it means to be powerful, I thought.

"It's past ten, isn't it?" I asked.

"Each party waits in one of these rooms until everyone has arrived. They're all scanned thoroughly while they wait, and when the last one arrives, they have to be scanned, too. We always start late."

"Who will be here?" I said.

"No one knows until we're in there," he answered. "Safer that way."

After a few quiet minutes, the door slid open and we walked into the big Parthenon Room. Other figures were stepping out of doors along the two walls to my left, but I didn't look toward them, not wanting to act like a newbie. Instead, I observed the room ahead of me. In its middle was a huge table with numerous extensions reaching out to the thick chairs around it. It was cleverly engineered to make each of its occupants feel that he was sitting together on the same board, while still retaining a sense of individuality.

Paul gestured at a chair to the left of the one he was taking, and as I sat down in it, I noticed for the first time that Saul was already seated to Paul's right, with the massive bodyguard standing silently behind him. Not wanting to meet the old man's eyes, I resumed my study of the room, taking in the two far walls in front of me, which were made of transteel and afforded an impressive view of the city's lights.

The transteel was punctuated by a series of ornate pillars, which extended all the way from the floor to the high-vaulted ceiling. The pillars also lined the two opaque inside walls, combining with the proliferation of marble surfaces to make the room fit its name. They also served a utilitarian purpose, because inside each one were components of the most sophisticated communications-jamming system ever developed. In surveillance terms, the system rendered this room one of the most quiet and invisible places on the planet.

"Welcome, men," Saul said after everyone was seated, and I briefly glanced around to see that the colorful group was indeed entirely male. I wondered if this was the case only this time, or if the old man refused to invite women leaders to these summits. I looked at him, feeling a cold sweat start to break out across my skin, because my quick look had given me the impression that most of the guests were looking at me. Perhaps it was just my imagination, however, because Saul went on as if I weren't there, diving straight into business without any pleasantries whatsoever.

He announced that there were two new innovations from the Sabon technology that he wanted to demonstrate for them, and the first was our recent combat test of the bugs during the tunnel assault. For a moment, I thought he might refer to me at this point, but he merely introduced a holographic report on the bugs' performance, which appeared suspended above the center of the table and was quite impressive in its production values. I did notice, however, that the producers conveniently left out the part about our casualties and the hidden compartments the bugs had failed to find on their first pass.

I already knew about what the holo was depicting, and I knew that the guests would be watching it intently. So I took the opportunity to survey these men who exercised singular authority in their respective realms, since the age of the global net had elevated corporations to the level of nations and turned nations into corporations with very little pretense of democracy. They were all watching the holo with appropriate interest, and none of them wore the proud look one would expect from a man who ruled millions.

The trip to the castle had a way of humbling them, as the old man had told me once. They came in by helicopter or ground car, as the aero technology they *did not have* swirled all around them. And the castle itself filled their vision with a reminder that Saul Rabin exercised a degree of control over his small kingdom that they would probably never enjoy in their big ones. Money talks, also, and each of these guests was paying an astronomical fee to BASS for the privilege of attending this one meeting.

The first individual visitor who drew my attention was by far the most important. General Zhang Sun (pronounced "soon") sat almost directly across the table from me, but I could see him under the bottom of the holo. The heads of the two thick bodyguards standing behind him were obscured by the holo, but I could tell that they were creations similar to Min, though not as big. Their presence spoke of the importance of the Chinese leader, because all the other guests had been required to leave their bodyguards in the waiting rooms. It also implied the prowess of Min, because the old man would certainly not have left himself at a disadvantage in protection. Apparently the combination of Cyber Hole and Silicon Valley artistry had made our machine-man a match for at least two of theirs.

Sun sat upright, his back not touching the chair. He wore a dark three-piece suit with a white shirt and tie—a style that had been in vogue a generation earlier. This was strangely symbolic of the "sleeping giant" quality that had left China playing catch-up with the West for a long time. Although the current premier of the Chinese Empire was a woman (a symbol that they had begun to catch up), those in the know were aware that she was merely a figurehead compared to this man, who exercised the real power.

While I was studying him, the Chinese general slowly

rotated his head toward me and met my eyes. And though his stone face remained utterly expressionless, I felt an almost extrasensory impression that he was directing aggression toward me, or even hatred. It may have been my imagination, again, or a form of paranoia, brought on by my fears in the current situation. But he did hold my gaze for what seemed an abnormally long time, before his head swung unhurriedly back to its former position.

To my left was Oscar Otero, the CEO of Macrosoft. He stole my attention away from Sun when he hoisted a pair of cowboy boots up to the edge of the table in front of him and rested them there, while he reclined farther in his big chair. Above the boots were a pair of well-worn blue jeans, and above the jeans was a new and ridiculously expensive Hanprin shirt, stretched over his muscular but aging torso. I didn't know too much about him, but I remembered that he had once been a soldier like me, with real combat experience.

To his left was Stanford Glenn, considered by many the most influential leader in the American Confederation. America was similar to China in that its president was a woman, but it was said that the buck stopped with this man. His black skin seemed even darker in contrast with his bright white sweater with a high collar, and the whites of his eyes. He had been a professional athlete, like D, and I think they had known each other fairly well. Also, like my dead friend, Glenn was tall and built well, even into his fifties. His official title was Foreign Statesman, a combination of the old offices of Secretary of State and Minister of Foreign Affairs. And in that office lay his power, because in the global economy of "spaceship earth," the survival and prosperity of nations depended on their relationship with the rest of the world. This was especially true of the AC, ever since the semi-decentralization of the government and the loss of big resources like the Bay Area, plus the rise of China and a consolidated Europe. I also remembered hearing that Stan Glenn's position was crucial to retaining Mexico as a part of the confederation and keeping its people from causing the problems they had before their assimilation.

The next guest I studied was C. T. Tamois, who looked androgynous as usual in his multicolored robe. This Frenchman had been raised in Geneva, the capital of the European Confederacy (or Europia, as it was more commonly known). It occurred to me that the countries of the Continent didn't have to worry about electing leadership to represent both sexes—Tamois did this himself.

Between Tamois and Sun sat a tiny Japanese man with a big head who looked like some kind of dwarf (perhaps as a result of Japan's renowned genetic experimentation). He wore eyeglasses, which had to be the old kind with no hardware, and he was listening to the holo through a translation program projected from the table that slightly distorted the air in front of him. This was peculiar, because the rest of the guests were not making use of theirs; obviously they all spoke Western quite well. Paul must have noticed my puzzled look, because he leaned over to me.

"Reality G," he whispered. "They call him a vice president, but he's the son of the guy who started the company. Nakamura is his name."

"He doesn't speak English?" I asked.

"I'm sure he does," Paul answered. "It's probably just an eccentricity, or a way to get some attention. He and the Brit are slightly out of their league here." He leaned away, and as he did, I saw "the Brit" for the first time, and gagged on my next breath.

To Saul's right was the last guest, and I knew instantly that he was here for my benefit (or my detriment, to be more precise). Howard Carter was merely the defense minister of England, a position that gave him less power than the prime minister, and *much* less than the king.

And there was no way that anyone in my former country could possibly have rated this kind of tryst. It was true that since returning political authority to the monarchy, Noel I had used his personal charisma and NATO connections to form the King's Alliance with threatened nations like Australia, India, Egypt, Canada, and finally Taiwan. But even this miraculous revival of the old British Empire did not place England on the map with the others in this room. No, the only reason Carter could possibly be here was to incite me in some way—because we hated each other with a bloody passion. So much so that he was one of the primary reasons I had left my home country almost ten years earlier.

Saul Rabin knew all this, of course, so I couldn't help glaring at him when the holo ended, ignoring Paul's preparatory warnings for a few moments. I felt the almost unnatural aggression rise within me again, which was like an itch that could be scratched only by personal violence. I wondered if this might be a residual effect from the use of the neural implant, or a harbinger that it was about to be used. I imagined losing consciousness and waking up in the cathedral, finding out that I had pounced across the table and viciously strangled a world leader.

But nothing happened, yet, except that the old man began a personal sales pitch about the new technology. He seemed not to have noticed my glare, so I looked down as he spoke, not wanting to push my luck.

18

"As you heard, men—" Saul seemed to relish pointing out the masculinity of the group, "the only weakness in this early stage of development is the limitation of the power source. Once we extend their life—and you can bet they will get smaller, too—they will be the *ultimate* in surveillance equipment. As the report said, but I can't help repeating it, 'For all those times you wish you could be a fly on the wall—now you can!' Isn't that good?"

He seemed genuinely pleased with himself—a rare moment for the old crank.

"Now, you know we could help you with that," the Macrosoft chief, Otero, spoke up, in the drawl that was often referred to as Tex-Mex. As everyone looked at him, he stretched his hands back and clasped them behind his head, looking too relaxed to be truly relaxed. As evidence of this, the boots soon came down off the table, and the hands back to his lap. "Size is everything, of course, in our research. And that includes power sources." For some reason, he squinted across the table at the stiff Chinese. "Have you seen the new 'light dot' we're pushing?" Sun didn't so much as blink, so Otero looked back over at the older Rabin. "That thing will last for six months."

A few seconds of silence ensued as Saul waited for someone else to speak. No one did.

"I don't know, Oscar," he prodded, "what would our other friends think about a partnership between two such heinous monopolies?" He then kept his smile fixed on the broad-shouldered CEO, but remained quiet for a while.

"I would think," Sun finally spoke up, with only the slightest accent, "that such collusion might heighten the suspicions about the Far West that are being entertained by many from the other nations." He looked at Glenn and Tamois, in that order. Then he looked at Otero and smiled, quite charmingly. "They are already quite convinced that when they look at a net display, you are staring back at them. That's why net rooms seldom have heads in them." This produced some chuckles from Tamois and Nakamura, and then finally Otero himself grunted in amusement, and returned his boots to the table.

Apparently the discussion was over, because the old man began introducing the next demonstration.

As he did, the table and chairs we were occupying began sliding away from the transparent wall, and from the hole that was left in the floor rose another, similar section with two men standing on it. As if that weren't impressive enough, a transteel barrier slowly emerged from the floor between us and the men, protecting us from them but allowing us to view them clearly. It was then I noticed that one of them wore body armor, while the other gripped an assault weapon.

"I wish we had this application of the Sabon technology back when I was a street cop," Saul said. "Watch the unarmed man as he activates his Atreides Shield—named after the man in the twentieth century who first conceptualized this."

The armored man manipulated something on his right hip, and soon there was a shimmering distortion in the air around his entire body. He stood still and watched as the other man raised his gun and fired directly at him for at least five seconds. Every one of the barrage of rounds either bounced off harmlessly or became embedded in the outer perimeter of the nearly invisible barrier, safely away from the protected man. From the location of the suspended bullets, we saw how he would have been struck in the head or chest had he not been wearing the shield.

After the firing was over, the old man proudly explained this phenomenon.

"The shield operates on the same antigravity system as the aeros, the falcons, our elevators, and the bugs, of course. And most of you have heard my very unscientific illustration of the principle, right? The one about holding an inflated ball under the water, letting go, and watching it pop up? The Sabon system works this way, on a molecular level, of course. But back to the shield . . . Our people have found a way to slave the system to a human body, as you see. So the shield repels anything heading toward it, much like it pushes against gravity and air in our flight system.

"In this proto version, however, until we perfect the limits of the system, the wearer has to maintain a careful balance and use the shield strategically." He gestured to the shimmering man, who remained standing still, the frozen bullets hanging in front of him. "If he turns the antigravity level up too high, it will dissipate outward."

The man reached toward his hip, where there seemed to be a hole or "pocket" in the shield, so that he could access the controls. He set the level higher, and the suspended pieces of lead suddenly flew away from him, scattering on the floor.

Saul continued. "But it also presses inward, which is why he's wearing body armor underneath the shield. He would be in considerable pain at this point if he wasn't, because for some reason we haven't yet been able to set acceptable limits without disrupting the system. But it won't be long before we have it perfected, of course." The armored man reached into the pocket and tuned the shield to a more comfortable level.

"The mobility of the wearer is also proportional to the intensity of the shield, as you could guess. At this level, where it was set for the demonstration you just saw, movement will be considerably hindered." The man illustrated this by moving around sluggishly for a few moments. "But you would be utterly impervious to projectiles, even explosive ones. On the other hand, when the shield's intensity is lowered, you can move very freely, but would have to avoid the bigger guns."

On cue, the man with the shield adjusted it so that he

could dodge the other man, who came at him with an eight-inch knife. After showing us how quickly he could move, he let the attacker stab hard and repeatedly at his chest, with no effect. At each thrust, the shield retreated ever so slightly, but then it pushed the blade back out before it could do any harm.

"As you can see, men," the Mayor said as the room began to revert to its original arrangement, "further Sabon development will not only be able to get us to new places, like outer space—but it will also protect us when we're there."

"And it could equip a formidable army. Or several of them." This pleasant voice came from the translation grid in front of Nakamura, the Reality G executive. Obviously, this translation program worked much better than the one in my glasses.

"What are you implying, Mr. Nakamura?" the old man responded, after a pause.

"I am more concerned about what *you* are implying," the dwarfish man answered.

"I'm afraid I don't follow."

"I am concerned about the reason for this protest we have seen."

"Demonstration," Oscar Otero said to the translation grid.

The Japanese man looked at him oddly for a moment, probably because he heard the same word he had just said returning to him, through the program. But then he realized what was going on, and he turned off the translation grid with his mind. The holo disappeared, and the only movement Nakamura had made was a brief fluttering of his eyelids.

Apparently the man could control the translation program, and who knew what else, with the cyberware inside his head. As I thought about this, it occurred to me for the first time that Saul himself might be wearing such equipment, and if so, he might be able to activate the chip in my head merely by thinking about it. Was this his plan, to wield me like a tool at some point during this meeting? Would he use me to silence an opponent who asked pesky questions, as Nakamura was about to do? Or did he have something more subtle, and more insidious, in store for me . . . ?

I shook my head, trying to quell my paranoia and replace the racing thoughts by focusing on the conversation that had begun at the table. A controversy was brewing there, about whether or not the old man was a Nazi.

19

“Are you threatening us with the military technology you are developing?” Nakamura said, obviously able to speak English just fine without the translation program. “Or are you trying to sell it to us?”

“Does it have to be one or the other?” Saul answered with an expression that indicated he was not taking the man entirely seriously. This seemed to fluster the tiny Asian, and the cheeks on his disproportionate head were turning more red than brown. I supposed this was because of a perceived loss of honor, or simply the same nervous emotion that I was feeling in this kind of company. He was probably new to this, like I was, and so I felt a pang of sympathy for the little man. Or I may have been just looking for another excuse to despise the Mayor.

"Maybe I want to see *who* will be threatened by it," the old man continued. "Or who *wants* to buy it." He kept his gaze on the Japanese man. "Or who will try to steal it."

"Or maybe you're a Nazi who wants to take over the world, like they say," Oscar Otero said with a chuckle.

"A 'nutzie'?" Saul said. That was how the Macrosoft chief had pronounced it. "Oh, a Nazi. What our critics say about us. Crushing freedom under our boots for the sake of security and progress, and so forth. That is utterly inane, of course; it reveals an embarrassing ignorance of history." He grunted and looked at the European leader in the multicolored robe. "Charlemagne, you are familiar with the history of your continent. Tell everyone how much Hitler and I have in common."

"Well, I have to admit," said the androgynous guest, "there are some similarities."

Out of the corner of my eye, I saw the old man's head retreat slightly, but he said nothing.

"The Führer believed in using the rule of law to enforce his ideological perspective," Tamois explained. "And his martial government did practice extreme prejudice with criminals, as you do."

"I hope you're not planning to conquer your neighboring countries, Saul," Stan Glenn said with a twinkle in his eye.

"Thank you, no," the older Rabin said, matching the American leader's levity, but then turning more serious. "Everyone believes in using the rule of law to enforce their ideology. You should know that, Charlemagne. What else are laws for?"

The multicolored man raised his eyebrows, squinted his eyes, and turned his head slightly.

"To preserve freedom," was his answer, but it sounded more like a question compared to the confidence in the old man's voice.

"What is freedom?" Saul Rabin said. He looked around the table for a moment, but no one spoke up. "If you say that every citizen is free to have his own ideology, that itself is an ideology. And you'll have to enforce that ideology with laws, if you want people to be able to live by it. I am not like Hitler, nor do I like Hitler—but not because he 'enforced his ideology.' I don't like Hitler because I do not agree with his ideology." His gaze now went back to Tamois.

"Double-talk," blurted the dwarf from Reality G. Then he looked to his right for some support. Otero shrugged, Glenn smiled weakly, and Tamois shuffled in his seat. My sympathy for Nakamura was now being replaced by resentment, because he was making all of us uncomfortable. Or was some virtual hand rearranging my brain to get me primed for murdering the little mutant? I found myself thinking how I could possibly pull it off, and wondering whether Min, or Sun's big bodyguards, would try to stop me. I even briefly scanned the table area for blunt instruments, until I realized how foolish this was and forced myself to focus on the conversation again.

The Mayor was waxing eloquent about the nature of freedom. "How much freedom does a train have when it has no tracks?" he was asking rhetorically. I had heard all this before from him, and back then it had been impressive, because he treated me so well, and I didn't particularly like the kinds of people he was criticizing. But now this self-righteous hot air just grated on me; I wanted to spare the world from ever having to hear it again. And whether he was Hitler to his subjects was irrelevant—he was already Brutus to me.

"Mr. Tamois also mentioned the summary-execution privilege." Zhang Sun said this from the left of the dwarf, abruptly changing the subject. His choice of words to describe the BASS policy was more than ironic. Yes, we did allow our peacers to use lethal force at their discretion, and three-time offenders faced the threat of capital punishment, either on the street or in the cathedral. But "summary execution" sounded so cruel and unforgiving that it effectively cut through the facade of decency created by our PR people. And to call killing criminals a "privilege" was too coincidental, coming from the only other leader at the table who would condone such a policy.

"Yes, and as I've always said," Saul responded, "deadly force can be good or bad, depending on who uses it."

Sun just nodded, and I stared at him, beginning to wonder if the old police chief and the Chinese warlord might have more in common than just their martial manner. If the Sabon technology of this West and the cyber technology of that East were married along with the latter's military, the amount of power they could wield together would be staggering. So maybe there *was* a world-domination plan going on here. Perhaps the allusion to the German fascist, who allied himself with a massive army from the East, was not so far off after all. . . .

Zhang Sun once again turned his head slowly to meet my

gaze, then looked away. But I felt the same sense of aggression emanating from him, even though his face remained blank. I thought that perhaps he knew of my role in the Taiwan crisis, but even that didn't seem capable of eliciting this kind of personal hostility. But as I reminded myself one more time, it might have just been my imagination.

"One could say that San Francisco is almost heaven," Saul Rabin was saying. "Because there are no lawyers in San Francisco, and we all know that there are no lawyers in heaven." The lightning scar on his cheek crinkled slightly from his thin smile, and he looked at Stanford Glenn. "By that standard, what would we call your country?"

"Hell on earth," the black man in the white sweater answered.

"Is being a lawyer a capital crime now in the Bay Area?" the Macrosoft man Otero said, stirred from his former indifference by the lighter spirit of the conversation.

Saul nodded. "We shoot 'em on sight," he said.

"I do not see what is humorous about any of this," Nakamura interjected. "Human rights are being violated in this 'heaven' of yours."

"Which rights are those, Mr. Nakamura?" the old man snapped back. "The right to avoid prosecution if you have enough money, or if the court system is too busy? The right to go on living while you are destroying the lives of others? Let me ask you a direct question, sir, since you are being so direct with me. What concern have your people shown for the countless thousands of human lives, especially young helpless ones, that have been sacrificed for the sake of your genetic experiments?"

"Tu quoque," Nakamura was quick to respond. "As Geneva affirmed, those experiments were morally acceptable because they have resulted in the greater good of our society."

"That sounds like Nazism to me," Paul said with a smile, which disappeared quickly when he caught a stern look from his father. So he added, "With all due respect, Mr. Vice President."

"By that standard," Saul spoke before anyone else could, "our experiment in justice has been successful on all counts. You will find no place in the world, with the exception perhaps of Mr. Sun's country, where the innocent feel more safe and the guilty feel more fear."

There was that connection between the Bay Area and China again. Were they birds of a feather, two fascist governments who would want to rule the world together?

"Of course, we could ask whether that is the standard which *should* be applied," Stanford Glenn said.

"True," Saul Rabin answered, appearing genuinely thoughtful. "But with the way the world has become, when other noble priorities seem to be so out of reach, so unrealistic . . . I suppose that safety and security have become among the most important ones to me." This moral dilemma seemed to engender in him a mild dose of humility, which was rare enough to cause a silence at the table for a few moments.

"Security," the old man repeated, then let out a tired breath. But then he suddenly snapped back into a business mode, and delivered the blow that I had been expecting all night, though it came in an unexpected form.

"Personal and national security is a concern we all have," he said. "And that is why I asked one of our executive peacers, Michael Ares, to tell you about the work he did in securing the Napa Valley a few years ago. He's prepared to share some insights that can revolutionize your own approach to protecting yourself and your people. Why don't you give that report I asked you to prepare, Michael?"

As the stares landed on me, I fought hard to not reward them with surprise or fear. Though his motives were a mystery, the old man had effectively strapped me into a no-win situation. I couldn't call him a liar, or even imply that he was mistaken, in front of these people, without committing an unforgivable faux pas. On the other hand, I had nothing to say, so the only alternative was to look like an unmitigated idiot.

I had thought that the Mayor might use me to perpetrate a political assassination—some kind of physical homicide. But now it seemed that he had planned a *professional* murder, and the victim was my career, and what was left of my reputation.

By now I was feeling nauseated, in addition to my acute exhaustion, and I longed to retreat into the bathroom for another splash of cold water, or perhaps to throw up. But instead I pressed a smile onto my face, tried to summon from my anger the motivation I needed to beat the old man at this mysterious game, and opened my mouth.

20

"I want to . . . um . . ." was all that I could get out before choking up and having to swallow, from nervousness and every other emotion that had been plaguing me. ". . . Say . . . something about Saul . . . Mr. Rabin."

"Are you all right, Michael?" the old man said abruptly, and the affront of his expressing concern for me jarred me enough to clear my mind, at least for the moment.

"When Mr. Rabin asked me to do this," I said, not looking at him, "I immediately began constructing an elaborate report, packed with information about the securing of the Napa Valley. But . . . then I remembered the kind of men to whom I would be reporting."

I raised my eyes and swung them around the table at the guests, who were all watching me curiously.

"I remembered that those of you who are interested in such

information would most likely have it already, and, uh . . . those of you who are not interested would not want to waste your precious time in such a manner." I looked at the old man now. "So, with your permission, I would simply like to answer any questions these men might have. If there are none, or few, you can then move on to more pressing matters."

Saul was now nodding repeatedly, mostly to himself, and it seemed more than just a response to my question. I looked around the table again at the guests, whose silence made my guess appear profound. Before I could conclude, however, one of them did speak up.

"I have a question *about* Mr. Ares," Stan Glenn said to the old man. "Though it's not related to the Napa Valley."

"By all means," Saul said, snapping out of his reverie.

"I'm concerned about the effect he may have on the stability of your organization," the black man said bluntly. "Whether there is any truth to the rumors that have been circulating."

"Do you want to know if the rumors are true, Stan?" said the Mayor. "Or do you want to know if they have a negative effect on BASS?"

"We could start with the first," Glenn answered.

Macrosoft's Otero, who had been studying his nails, brought his boots down off the table and sat up. The Chinese, on the other hand, remained statues.

"What rumors have you heard?" the old man asked. I was annoyed by the fact that I was clearly not a part of this conversation, but it didn't seem a good time to say so.

"Speculation that he killed the man above him, and his own child in the process."

The words stung me, but I tried not to move.

"Severe accusations, I know," Glenn continued, "but they seem to rise above the usual trash from the media. And that man named Harris, who hinted at this publicly, died in an assault led by Mr. Ares himself. That only heightens the suspicion that he may have committed the murders."

The old man knitted his brow and stared at the American until he was sure of his seriousness, then he turned to me.

"Is this true, Michael?" he asked. "Did you do this?"

Everyone looked at me.

"Yes," I said. "In a way."

Everyone looked at me more, and I sensed Paul shifting in his seat.

Then, to the old man, I said, "But you are also responsible."

Saul's only reaction was a slight smile, which I couldn't decipher. He met my eyes, and I let a few moments pass, during which I could tell that Paul was trying to decide whether or not to say something.

Then I added, to the whole table, "We both brought them into this dangerous lifestyle, so we both put them in harm's way."

I dropped my head, a despondent and guilt-ridden father and friend.

Paul relaxed in his seat, and then broke the silence.

"Of *course* there is no truth to those accusations," he said.

"If there were, we would be the first to deal with it. You should know that, Mr. Glenn."

"Why didn't you answer the claims on the net?" the black man asked after nodding in resignation.

"Haven't you ever read Shakespeare? 'The lady doth protest too much, methinks'?" Paul smiled warmly at the man, to soften his words. "Better to ignore it than sink to their level and look more guilty."

"We haven't heard anything from you, Mr. Rabin." This British voice came from Howard Carter, my accursed former boss. I looked up at him as he continued. "You don't seem highly confident in your man here." He gestured at me with his head, but wouldn't meet my gaze.

"Well," the old man said, examining the top of his cane for a few moments, as if for no other reason than to make us wait. "Michael is like a son to me." Then he leveled his gaze at Carter. "I would die for him."

"Ah," Carter said, nodding. "Yes." And the discussion was over.

You're gonna die for me tonight was all I could think as I watched the old man, who concluded the meeting and dismissed us without acknowledging me again. This bizarre episode had been the last item on the agenda, which strengthened my suspicion that it was actually the main reason for the whole meeting. Try as I might, I could not fathom why this would be, so I gave up trying on my way out of the Parthenon Room.

I collected the boas, exchanged a meaningful look with Paul, and headed to my office to wait for his call.

• • •

Safely situated in an office chair that cost more than most offices, and staring through the transparent wall at my twentieth-floor view of the city, I realized again how wasted I was, physically and emotionally. I turned on the chair's relaxor, hoping it would help a little, and it did. I remembered years before, when I used to keep a few confiscated Artstim derms in one of my desk drawers, and wished I had one now. Recalling why I had finally flushed the drugs down the toilet, I thought of Lynn, and tried to contact her again. The glasses were in my jacket, but I used the office, which doubled as a net room, so that anyone who answered could see my pitiful, yearning face.

Lynn's three numbers yielded nothing but messages again, but I did reach two of her closest friends, one in L.A. and the other here in the Bay Area. The bad news was that they both said they had not heard from her, but the good news was that they both seemed to be telling the truth. This meant that she might have gone home, and simply wasn't answering the phone.

I glanced at a clock and noticed it was almost 1:00 A.M. That meant I had about three hours before I would have my chance to confront the murderer of my friend and daughter—or the *other* murderer, I should say. On top of the resident exhaustion and nausea, I felt a pang of fear and another ache in my head where I imagined the neurochip was located. I wondered if I could make it three hours before it was activated again, to cause me to perpetrate another craven deed or to burn out half my brain.

I selected a holo on the player in my desk. I needed to be doing something in case I was being watched, because I wanted to replace the stopper rounds in my right boa with killers. When the holo came on, I began to do this, without being able to see my hands or the gun, as I watched my wife and daughter fly a kite in the park. Grass and sky and the sound of wind were all around me. I had made this holo not too long ago with my glasses, and seeing it now hurt worse than my physical pain. But it brought flashes of pleasure, too, and after I was finished reloading the gun, I slumped into the comfort of the chair and enjoyed what I had lost.

After Lynn managed to get the kite in the air, and the string secured in Lynette's hand, she backed over to me and slid her arm around me. I almost felt her against my side as I studied her face close-up, taking in the combination of stunning profile and imperfect skin, both of which were highlighted by the bright morning sun. I looked back at my little girl, who had stopped yelling, "I'm doing it!" and now wasn't sure what she should do next. I broke off from Lynn and walked to Lynette, encouraging her with a hug that brought near her features, which were a gorgeous fusion of mine and her mother's. Then I told her to run with the kite, because it was starting to descend. She ran the wrong way, of course, and soon we had to relaunch it.

In the bright light of this virtual reality, my hand came up to wipe the tears from my eyes, which were caused by the allergy-inducing winds of the Napa Valley. And in the darkness of real reality, my hand was also wiping my eyes. . . .

The phone rang, Paul's voice came on, and soon I was entering Saul Rabin's top-floor lair, noticing that it seemed darker and more ominous than ever before. Out of a swirling mist of atmospheric chemicals, the old man appeared, leaning on a pulse rifle instead of his cane. He laughed maniacally.

"Come to kill me before I kill you?" he spat, then began to raise the big gun so slowly that it wasn't even a threat.

"You killed my daughter, you bastard!" I screamed, and emptied both boas into him. There was no blood on his body as it fell to the floor.

"You killed my father," Paul said as he emerged from the mist. I realized my guns were spent, and wondered if I could take the big man in hand-to-hand combat. But before I could decide on a course of action, his frown turned to a smile, and he added, "And I'm glad you did!"

He moved forward and embraced me, which was unpleasant because he seemed to be enjoying it too much. I started to pull away, but before I could, a wall of brown flesh twice our size dropped from the ceiling and knocked us to the ground.

Min picked up both of us, since we were still stuck together, and threw us across the room effortlessly. We bounced off the hard floor and flew apart, landing in separate places. I was still conscious, but could move only my head, so I turned it toward them, wiping the floor with my face. I watched as Paul's crumpled form straightened out on the floor, then stood up as if he hadn't been injured at all. He stood next to Min, and smiled as the big cyborg activated a disk bomb and slid it across the floor toward me.

It lodged under my lame side, and I waited for it to blow. I could not will myself to move, but I was able to feel the bomb vibrating on and off, as if it was counting down toward detonation. . . .

I awoke in total darkness, and it took me a few moments to realize that the holo had ended and the glasses in my jacket were buzzing against my side, where the vibrating bomb had been in my dream. I groped for the glasses and slid them on before they stopped. It was the old man, calling from the top floor.

"Michael, are you there?" he said.

"Yes," I answered.

"Oh, good. Paul just told me that you have some questions for me, that you'd like to have a talk."

"Yes," I said, trying to gather myself. "Is that all right?"

"Yes, of course. Come on up."

I turned off the holo player, and the darkness disappeared. I was back in my office, and it was just after four. I felt for the boas, to make sure they were there, and as I touched them I felt the simmering anger inside me flare up again. I wet my face again in the washroom, and left the office, hoping that destiny would postpone my inevitable physical collapse, and any tampering with my brain, until I could taste my sweet revenge.

21

I rode a horizontal lift, walked a hallway, submitted to a security scan, and stepped inside the private elevator to the penthouse. The elevator was on the outside of the building, facing north, so I stood facing the night cityscape as I began to ascend. Beyond the lights of the surrounding buildings, I saw the big dark blotch of the Bay, punctuated by the Golden Gate Bridges on the left and Alcatraz Island toward the right.

Despite my preoccupations, I was enjoying the view, because I usually couldn't see anything when I rode up to meet with the Mayor. Those meetings were most often in the late afternoon, when the sun filled the view side with an almost unbearable glare. I always had to turn around and face the door on the inside of the elevator . . .

Suddenly, I lost all interest in the panorama.

I turned around, like I usually did when the sun was assaulting me, and searched the metal around the closed elevator door for a camera casing. There was one, of course—a small protruding square to the left of the door that was unnoticeable unless someone was looking for it.

I punched the button for the nearest floor, which was the twenty-first, and felt the elevator glide to a stop. I did not open the door or activate it by moving toward it, but stood thinking for a minute or more. Then I turned back around and stared at the city, and into the maw of the Bay, hoping this might grant me some clarity. Finally, I concluded that even if these new ideas invading my head were the result of full-blown delirium, or some kind of neurological manipulation, it still couldn't hurt to check them out—as long as it didn't take too long.

I selected a new floor, and the elevator started to descend. I brought my glasses out and slipped them on, auto-dialing a number that I should have taken out of my queue a long time ago.

I was greeted by a virtual version of my old flame, standing in the lobby of her apartment, with link icons hanging in the air all around her. "Hi, you've reached Tara's site," she said. "You can try to find me at home, at work," she gestured to the icons as she spoke, "or you can try my glasses." I moved the tiny mouse on mine until the glasses' icon was highlighted, then selected it.

Thankfully, she answered, on audio-only. "This is Tara."

"It's Michael," I said.

She didn't answer right away, but then: "Two times in two days. I'm a very lucky girl." I was silent, because I was still formulating a plan to escape the reach of the old man's surveillance. If he had seen me stop the elevator, he definitely would be watching me closely. "What do you need?" she asked.

"I need you," I answered, making up my mind. Now the silence on the other end was tangible. "Where are you right now?"

"At the office," she answered.

There is a God, I thought. She was still doing half her work in the early hours of the morning, so that she could leave early.

"Stay right there," I said, already moving in her direction. I removed the glasses, thinking that she was my special angel—not because I wanted her so much but because she still loved me. And that made her someone I could trust, at least to a good degree.

The Internal Security floor was almost empty, of course, because of the hour. As I approached Tara's office, I pushed out of my mind a few memories of other times like this, and opened the door. She stood in the center of the room, wide-eyed. I closed the door behind me and approached her, slipping my arms around her and pulling her close. I put my mouth right at her ear, where only one human being could hear what I was saying.

"I'm sorry, Tara," I whispered, and felt her soften in my arms. I then realized that wasn't the best way to start, because she was probably thinking that I regretted leaving her for Lynn.

"This isn't what it seems," I continued. "But you must, absolutely *must,* act like it is." Her body tensed again. "Someone may be watching me. They want to kill me, and I need your help. Can you pretend that you're in love with me for a few minutes?"

I gave her a moment to struggle with her emotions, but held her so that she couldn't pull away.

She finally whispered in my ear, "I don't have to pretend."

I asked her to access the security tapes from the penthouse elevator, find a time when I was riding it in the late afternoon, and bring me a still shot. I told her I would wait for her here, and as I said all this, I moved my head back and forth periodically between her right and left ears, and swayed slightly to make it look like we were sharing a tender moment. When I was done, she pulled away from me reluctantly.

"I have to check something on the equipment," she said, wiping a tear from her eye, and stepping to the door. "I'll just be a minute. Wait for me, okay?"

"Forever," I said, overdoing it.

She fought more tears and left the office. I waited, and in just a few minutes she was back, nothing in her hands.

"I've missed you," she said as she came close again.

"It hasn't been that long," I said, putting my arms around her again.

"Oh yes it has," she answered, and began to position us subtly so that her back was to the one camera. She slipped off her shoes and lowered herself, so that the front of her shirt was now hidden from the other camera by my shoulders. Then, from inside the shirt, she slid a small printed image, which she held with her one hand against the brown skin below her neck. I nuzzled her cheek and looked down at the picture.

It was almost identical to the one that had been taken out of D's head, according to Paul. My silhouette, with a bright glow filling the background. I remembered Paul saying that he knew how to work the surveillance system in the penthouse, and I realized that he could easily have captured that still anytime I had ridden the elevator to meet with the old man.

I managed to gently transfer the image from Tara's hand to a pocket inside my jacket, while still enjoying her embrace. I asked her in a whisper if she was able to turn on the top-floor cameras from here, and she told me no. Then I pulled away slightly, though still grasping her hand.

"Thank you," I said.

"No, thank *you*," she answered predictably. I turned away, but she held on to my hand until she had to let go.

I thought of Lynn and left the office.

"Uncle Paul! Uncle Paul!" my little Lynette was saying, on her knees at the window in the backseat of Darien's car. She was excited to see my friend there, at the city house, as he walked in through the open gate in front of the car. D himself thought this was unusual, but nonetheless started to lower the passenger-side window to find out why his boss had come to see him. Paul suddenly blurred into action, but before D could react, he and his passengers were meeting their maker in a deafening eruption of fire, metal, and blood.

The scene was playing differently now in my mind as I rode the elevator back up to the penthouse—but I didn't want to believe it. A new swirl of emotions had obscured the focused anger that had been sustaining me, and now I felt more tired and sick than ever. I was almost sure that I would be dying tonight, and wondered if I was ready. The only thing I was sure about was that I wanted to see Lynn again—even more now that I felt the abandoned hope of innocence clawing its way up through the pain inside me. But something else inside was telling me that I was only kidding myself—creating a virtual reality that was not unlike the analgesic media in which the masses forget their crimes.

The elevator came to a halt, and the security scan ignored my boas, as it usually did, so I drew both of them out as I walked through the little room designed to keep the artificial atmosphere stable.

I passed through the second set of doors and found myself in the big central room of the apartment. Unlike in my dream, there were no mists, only a different feel to the air that was hard to identify or describe. It *was* rather dark, however, and sparsely decorated. The old man had not brought over any of the furnishings from the house he had shared with Mrs. Rabin, presumably because he didn't want such reminders of their life together. Instead, the furniture in his new residence was strictly utilitarian, utterly lacking a woman's touch. It occurred to me that my life would be like this, without Lynn.

"Have you come to me with swords and clubs?" a voice said from the shadows to my right. It was the old man's, no doubt quoting some of the ancient literature he was so fond of.

I moved toward the voice and saw that he was leaning on his cane, in front of the transteel wall, which was darkened so that the lights of the city shone only dimly behind him. Nonetheless, there was enough light behind him to make him appear as a mere shadow, until I stepped closer and saw his face. The big scar stood out more in the half-light, and he seemed to be unarmed.

"Where's Paul?" I asked, stopping about six feet away from him, and holding the boas ready.

"In his quarters," he said, and gestured across the big room to one of its many doors. I saw that a light was on behind the door, and it seemed likely that someone on the other side of it could hear what we were saying, if he wanted to. I moved to my right, so that I could see the door, but kept the same distance from the old man.

"Why are you pointing your guns at me, Michael?"

"Because I'm about to kill you," I answered, straining my overtaxed mind to guess at the best approach to this mess.

"Forever why?" asked the old man.

I looked in his eyes. *Windows to the soul,* they say.

"Did you put a chip in my head and make me kill people?"

"What?"

"Did you surgically implant cyberware in my brain to control me?"

"What?"

"Is there an echo in here?" I said, glancing around and then down at the boas. "Answer the question."

" 'Heavens no' is the answer," he said. "But the *question* you should be asking is, who wants you to think that. Where did you get the idea?"

Not wanting to mention Paul yet, I told him that my investigation had uncovered a black op called Mind Lift, and moved my index fingers to the insides of the trigger guards for the first time as I studied his response.

"Well, my son wanted to do the mind-control thing," he said sadly, "when my Legacy Project was first being developed. He called it Mind Lift initially, then changed it to Romans something, in an attempt to make it more palatable to me . . . because of his mother, I suppose." He sighed. "But Paul was always misusing the Good Book. So when I found out what it was, I pulled it from him, put the previous research under wraps, and kept it pointed in the right direction."

"So you're claiming that there's nothing in my head?"

"Oh, I wouldn't say that, Michael. You're a very intelligent man, though perhaps a bit naive. But that's typical for someone who started out military, rather than police, and I think you're being cured of that." He smiled again, seeming much more relaxed than usual, but then turned serious. "No, really. BASS didn't actually *do* any of that, what you're asking about; I stopped it before it left the idea stage." Now he was looking at me sympathetically. "Besides, I don't think that kind of thing will ever happen."

"Why's that?" I asked, then realized that his calm manner had caused me to lower the guns slightly. When I brought my arms back up abruptly, I noticed that his hand tensed on the top of his cane, but didn't think any more of it at that point because he quickly relaxed again, and the smile returned.

"Well, two reasons. First, because the technology may not even be feasible without doing catastrophic damage to the brain. I don't understand the science of it very well, but I know some researchers are skeptical, because for decision and bodily action the parts of the brain work in global coordination to the extent that you would have to place integrated wetware all throughout the skull to control someone's choices. Or at least something that can move throughout, like nanotechnology far more advanced than we have so far."

He looked at me as if to gauge my understanding, then continued when I didn't say anything.

"All that's actually been proven is that communication of existing thought can happen between parts of the brain and cyberware, for the purpose of information exchange and manipulation of equipment by the brain, but not the other way around, except for the most rudimentary stimulation of the senses. No one's been able to actually create thought or cause complex action, which leads me to my second reason—"

"Paul mentioned something," I interrupted. "About a 'bridge' in the brain linking the parts." He nodded in response, and turned slightly toward the closed door to Paul's room, as if he was remembering that his son was on the other side of it.

"He knows much more about it than I do," was his answer. "As I told you, it was *his* thing, not mine. But I know it's nothing more than theory at this point, which leads me to—"

"What about Geneva?" I interrupted again, and he nodded again.

"The reason for Geneva was primarily the danger of 'mind reading,' which is possible with the tech we have, rather than the more theoretical 'mind control.' But they did go on to discuss the ethics of the latter, because of certain assumptions that I don't share, but which have to do with my second reason why what they fear will probably never happen." He paused and looked at me.

"What's your second reason?"

"I thought you'd never ask," he said with the wry smile and a little laugh. He seemed happier than I'd ever seen him before, like a crushing load he always carried had been lifted from his back.

"It's all based on a naturalistic misconception about human nature," he explained. "The brain doesn't determine what the brain does, as if we are merely physical beings. The mission-control center in Homo sapiens is the *mind*, otherwise known as the heart, the soul, the spirit, very subtle mind, jiva, et cetera. Choices of the will, meditation, conscience, worship, metaphysical desires—things like that all start with this immaterial part of us, which directs the brain, not the other way around . . . so you can't force someone to do something by manipulating their brain. The brain stores information which can be read or impaired, and bodily senses can be stimulated and simulated through it . . . so you could make it a lot harder for the mind or soul to make certain choices, maybe, but you can't *make* it decide something. No human being can, anyway."

"What do you mean, 'no human'? Are you talking about aliens now?"

"Well, if there was a being or beings whose realm was the spirit, or who were powerful spirits themselves," that wry smile again, "maybe they could."

Watching his eyes widen as he spoke of the supernatural,

I found myself growing more wary and tense again. Then he shifted his weight slightly and rested both hands on the top of his cane, and both of mine gripped the boas tighter as I realized why I had been subconsciously concerned about the walking stick. If what Paul had told me was true, then the old man himself might have implants that could trigger the chip in my head, or he might need external controls to do so. And the cane, being close to him at all times, would be ideal for such a purpose. I tried not to stare at the slight movements of his fingers or let paranoia overtake me, because he might have been merely adjusting his grip on the handle. But I imagined him manipulating a button and turning off my brain, or exploding it with another, and I made sure my index fingers were resting on my own triggers, in case the unthinkable occurred and I needed to take him with me.

"Is this a religious, a Christian thing?" I asked him.

"Not exclusively. Most early humanists were not naturalistic, and the basic idea of free will is something that's pretty popular with atheists and agnostics, too. I'll admit that I find the Edwardian explanation quite compelling, but that's rather obscure now . . . very few orthodox Christians are welcomed to the academic table these days, at least in the English-speaking world." He took his left hand off the cane again and scratched his ear with it, and my soldier/cop instincts told me this slight movement might be a diversion, so I fixed my eyes on the top of the black stick until he was done. But he continued talking without event. "Actually, most of the best work in this century has been done by Buddhists . . . the Dalai Lamas have been partnering with neuroscientists since the 1990s to prove the 'elasticity' of the brain, as they call it. Meditation practices can reshape the pathways of the brain . . . it's been documented time and again. No, Christianity is not the only worldview that elevates the mind over the brain." At this point he ruminated for a few seconds, then added, "Huh, ironic . . . There's the real mind lift, I think."

I stared at him, still holding the boas in front of me and trying to decide whether or not I needed to understand what he was talking about.

"You know I have killer rounds loaded in both of these," I said, nodding toward the guns. "I assure you that if you did something to my brain, they would still go off." I then nodded toward his cane, trying to appear much more sure about what I said than I actually was. Saul also looked down and nodded at the cane. Then I added, "Or do you have an implant yourself?" and directed my gaze back to his gray head.

"You *are* a decent detective, Michael," he said with another indecipherable smile. "And not far from the truth on both counts." His eyes looked down to the cane, then up toward his forehead.

My fingers pressed harder on the warm plasteel of the triggers.

"But I assure *you*," the old man continued, "that I could do no such thing, and would not, because I now believe that you will be our true peacer." His words puzzled me, but they felt genuine enough for me to loosen up a little. Only a little, though.

"Did my son tell you these lies about me?" he asked.

"Your son is my friend," I answered.

"Yes . . ." he said with a sigh. "And he is my son. But that does not leave me blind to his . . . weaknesses.

"Paul is two people, Michael," he continued. "One on the outside, and another on the inside."

"Aren't we all?" I said.

"No, not like him. You and I have dual natures, in a way, but we are both good and bad on the inside. They struggle against each other. But my son surrendered to the bad long ago, and he merely presents morality, compassion, loyalty, and friendship on the outside, to gain the power that he craves. There is a difference. He has no conscience—one of those faculties of the soul I mentioned—or his conscience has become thoroughly calloused. My responsibility, I must admit . . . God knows I've had to make many hard decisions, but I've never assumed they were right, and I know some were very wrong.

" 'It's good to be the king,' people say, but actually it's *hard* to be the king. Paul doesn't think in these terms at all, however; he just wants to rule. I realized this about him in recent years, about the same time I found out that I was dying. So I knew I had to do something about the future of BASS."

"You're dying?"

"I have a tumor in my brain." He nodded. "And out of over three hundred fifty types of cancer that have been identified, this is one of the dozen or so they still cannot treat effectively." He shook his head and exhaled a tired laugh. "And not long ago I realized that it would be a crime against the world if I left my son in charge of all this, though I do love him dearly. I began the process of rearranging my testamentary orders, so that the company would be decentralized upon my death. I was about to make you and Darien the primary officers, as soon as I was sure of your qualifications." I wondered what he meant by that last part, while he looked over at Paul's door, as if expecting the younger Rabin to emerge at any time. "Unfortunately, my son found out about my plans, and he's been trying to stop them." He lowered his head in shame, sadness, or both.

"So you're saying that Paul killed them?" I asked, and putting it into words made my legs feel weaker beneath me and the guns heavier in my hands.

"Once you jettison this 'neurocide' nonsense," he answered, "who else could have pulled it off?"

"So he's framing me for the murder," I said, more a statement than a question, because the truth had now fully dawned on me.

Images flickered through my mind, of Paul affirming his friendship over the years. Of Paul calling me the night Lynette died. Of Paul assuring me that we would find the killer. Of Paul telling me about the neurochip and the death image. Of Paul convincing me that the old man was responsible, and had lost it completely. Of Korcz saying that someone high up in BASS was rotten. Of Paul explaining how we had to quickly destroy his father, one way or another. Of Lynn questioning his word, and refusing to believe the worst about the older Rabin. Of Kim lying dead on the street. Of Paul contriving for me to be here, right now, so that I might take my "revenge."

"And he planned to kill both of us tonight," I finished.

"And I still do," came Paul's voice from behind the door as it was opening. I swung both of my guns around and locked them on the big man, who held two of his own and walked calmly toward us. "I was waiting and hoping, *Michael*, that you would put the old man out of his misery for me." He spat my name, like I had never heard it from him before. "But all you did was talk . . . and talk and talk . . . even a million-dollar drug couldn't diffuse your sickening limey loyalty, I suppose."

"You put it in my drink at the ranch," I said.

"Yeah, I bought it from a very happy Czech on the Continent. It's supposed to cause an initial fit of rage, and then raise your aggression level for about a week. Their military uses it. But obviously it didn't work as well as I'd hoped." He stopped the same distance from both of us, making a triangle.

"Oh, it worked," I said. "Only now I want to kill *you.*"

"Good luck," he said, smiling broadly, and for the first time I noticed that the air around his body was shimmering.

He was wearing one of the experimental shields, and now I was completely sure that I would be dying tonight.

22

“But the drug didn’t have to work, you see,” Paul contin-ued, proud of his devious machinations, and obviously able to put us away in his own good time. “They’ll find it in your body, and assume that you took it to prepare yourself for more murder and mayhem, which will fit the profile I’ve constructed.”

“Which is?” I asked, glad that he was talking while I frantically tried to figure a way out of this.

“You’re already under suspicion for murdering your superior, since I leaked a hint of that and the video clip to Harris. Even the *possibility* that you killed your own daughter to get ahead makes you look like a monster, or at least highly unstable. And why stop with Darien? Why not take out the Rabins as well? Chinatown security scanned your card today, and the cameras at Cyber Hole recorded you asking them when our bodyguard would be gone, with no official authorization. And beyond all that, I have a film of you from my home theater saying, 'I just killed three people, including my own daughter.'" He smiled even bigger at me. "You're history, man."

"Why would you do this, Paul?" the old man broke in, though his sad eyes said that he already knew the answer.

"Because like you said, I'm not going to let you take away my chance to be king." I wondered if he meant king of the Bay Area or king of the world, but I supposed that both would be true of the man who inherited BASS. "I grew tired of living in your shadow a long time ago, and then you bring in these two pretty boys to upstage me more. You *must know* what everyone, big or little, says about Paul Rabin: 'If the Mayor wasn't his father . . .'

"I'm taking no more of that," he finished. "Every knee will bow."

"Did you kill D and the kids yourself?" I asked.

"Oh yeah," he said, and I winced involuntarily. "The kids weren't a part of the original plan—they were just there when the best time came around. But we can't have witnesses, of course." He felt my glare, and added, "But if you hadn't dropped your daughter off that night, maybe she wouldn't be dead. So maybe you did kill her after all."

"And Kim?" I asked, ignoring his taunts.

"Who?"

"Kim, the tech we chased in the city."

"Oh, yeah. I sent a message to him that he knew too much and we were coming to kill him. That's why he ran. You almost did him in yourself when I told you the wrong fingers for the bird . . . that would have been even better, but at least you were seen all over the city chasing him, so if someone had to be tagged for his murder, it could be you. Then, when I found him, I slammed into him with the falcon when he was near the front of the trolley, and now he's resting in pieces." He shrugged apologetically for the joke. "But that was *really* fun. I've been wanting to do this kind of stuff for years, and those acting classes sure paid off. You were so snowed . . ."

"You obviously haven't turned on the cameras up here," I said.

"Give that man another degree!" he said sarcastically. "But enough talk. Now we're going to have a good old-fashioned gunfight, though it'll be somewhat one-sided. At the end, you'll both be dead—my beloved father and his killer, who I tried to stop."

I noticed for the first time that his two guns were boas, like mine, to make sure the ordnance evidence would not be an issue.

"I may even wound myself, for effect," he said with a shrug. "I haven't decided yet."

He waved the guns around for a moment, deciding whom to shoot first, then pointed one at each of us. "Goodbye, old man," he said to Saul.

"Goodbye, Paul," said the gray-haired man, and then made his move in an explosion of motion that was remarkably fast for a man of any age—especially his. He simultaneously threw his cane at Paul and jumped in front of me, clasping my shoulders in his hands and carrying me to the floor. Saul yelled, "Go, Michael!" as Paul instinctively fired both boas at our falling figures. As we neared the floor, I felt the impact of several bullets on the old man's body and was sprayed with blood from at least one exit wound, but I was not hit myself. Paul got off only a few rounds in this initial flurry, because Saul's cane had begun spraying a heavy gas while it was still in the air. From where I now lay, behind the old man's limp body, I saw the shielded man staggering back, unsure whether the gas would affect him.

Knowing I would die if I stayed in the room, and hoping I could escape Paul and return to Saul somehow, I made use of the momentary window of opportunity he had given me by thrusting myself up to my feet and sprinting to the door through which I had entered the room. I reached it before Paul noticed me, but was a sitting duck for the few long seconds it took for the door to slide open. So I crouched and fired at him repeatedly with the one boa I still held, hoping that the impact of my shots on his shield would at least distract him. As I did, the metal surfaces around me clanged and pinged and sparked like fireworks from his slugs, but somehow none of them connected with me before I had backed safely into the little room.

The door slid shut between us, absorbing his last few shots.

I remembered Saul's saying that a man moves more slowly with the shield level up, but I didn't know how slow, so I hurried through the second door to the elevator and mashed the first button I saw. The elevator rose to the roof, and just seconds later its door opened to the windy city air. Then it started to close again, so I quickly squeezed out onto the roof, not wanting to ride it back down toward Paul. I heard it start to descend, so I spun around to survey the roof.

About a hundred feet away, protruding from the surface, was the private entrance to the apartment that we had entered the night Lynette died. In front of it and slightly to the right sat an aero, which I assumed belonged to Paul. Beyond it was a big garden, and on the far side of the garden I knew there was another external elevator, similar to the one behind me.

I could hear the elevator behind me coming back up, so I had no time to weigh any options. I took off running as fast as my tired legs could take me, hoping to reach the shelter of the aero or the elevator housing before Paul shot me in the back. I could almost feel the door opening behind me before I reached my goal, but I pressed forward anyway with a few more bounding steps, then dived and rolled behind the aero. I jerked up into a crouching position, grabbed the back bumper, and peered around the edge of the car at the elevator.

The door was already open and Paul had emerged, the shield shimmering around him and the two guns pointed in my direction.

"I saw you, Michael, I know where you are," he said as he began moving toward me across the empty space on the roof. "The old man bought you a few extra minutes, but it won't make any difference. You can't move from there without me shooting you; you can't shoot me because of the shield. I have the only key to that aero here in my jacket, and even if you could get away somehow, you're now the most wanted man in the Bay Area. If you were actually captured rather than shot on sight, which is unlikely, no one would believe you against all the evidence, or take your word against mine." He was about halfway to me by now. "So just come out and take it like a man, please. Don't cower behind there. Don't make me shoot up that fine piece of machinery just to end your miserable life, when it's already over anyway."

Crouched against the back of the aero, I frantically studied the distance between me and the elevator housing, to see if I could somehow make it there alive. Paul was right . . . there was no way I could. And even if by some chance I did, it would only put me back down in the apartment again. Maybe if I reached the elevator, I thought, I could sabotage it and keep him out, but even then he could probably override the door or just wait until his helpers arrived. I couldn't think of any way out of this, so all I could do was raise my head and look through the rear window of the car to see how close he was. But when I did, my eyes were looking across the cover of the trunk, and a thought hit me.

Could it be? Maybe, because they are *his favorite toys. But would he have the same voice code on this aero as he did on the ground car? Maybe . . .*

I didn't have anything to lose, so I said "Interview!" toward the back of the car.

Nothing happened, except that Paul heard me and said "What?"

I pressed my eyes shut, trying to remember, and whispered, "Please God, please God . . ." Then it came to me.

"Wintermute?" I said, and immediately the trunk slid open.

"What?" Paul said again, then muttered, "Oh no," when he saw through the windows of the aero that I was reaching into the trunk with my one hand, and putting my glasses on with the other. There was only one in this car, rather than two, but the remote registered in the glasses and responded to my grip.

The falcon rose into the air above the car, its wings extending as it did. For a moment, Paul was frozen in awe at the sight of this frightening weapon pointing at him rather than someone else. I squeezed the remote with all my fingers at once, unleashing a barrage of killers, stoppers, and gas pellets in his direction. Then I ran for the nearby elevator, knowing that the car, the bird, and the gas were filling the space between me and Paul, who was stumbling backward with his arms up from the attack. When I was in the elevator and the door had closed, I saw through the falcon's view in my glasses that Paul had recovered enough to start shooting at it—neither the bullets nor the gas I fired had penetrated the shield. So I swung the bird back and to the right, keeping it away from Paul and mobile enough to make it hard for him to hit.

I was enjoying this inverted version of skeet until I noticed the red line from the elevator's security system start at the ceiling and proceed slowly down the walls toward my head. I felt a surge of fear and crouched instinctively, realizing afterward that I did this because Paul might have changed the security codes to exclude me, in which case I would soon be "resting in pieces," to use his expression. I said, "Please God," again, this time just in my mind, and rather involuntarily. The red line reached my head and then traversed down my body for an agonizing five seconds, but nothing happened except that the elevator came to a stop and the door opened.

As I stepped through the small anteroom and then through the second door into the penthouse's big middle room, I continued watching the roof in my glasses and firing on Paul with the falcon, pulling it back and swinging it around him in wide arcs when he shot back. I noticed he was moving in reverse toward the other elevator, which meant he would be coming my way soon, and I didn't have much time down here. So I ran over to Saul and knelt down by him, while trying to occupy Paul with the falcon as much as I could.

The old man's body lay riddled with bullets, a few of which had hit him when he was acting as my shield, and others that Paul had added afterward to make sure he was dead. I was hoping that he might have survived, so that he could somehow assist me and both our lives could be saved. But all I could do was close his eyes and give him a brief message, which consisted mostly of "sorry" and "thank you." Then I had to go, because I saw through the falcon's view that Paul had reached the elevator and was now inside it, riding it back down to the penthouse. I couldn't survive a close-quarters battle with him, especially while he was armed, but a last desperate plan was coming together in my mind.

As I took my body back the way I'd come in, I brought the falcon into my elevator through the roof entrance and down to the penthouse level. I took its place in the elevator and sent it into the penthouse while I stayed in the safety of the elevator. Paul was halfway through the big room, looking for me, when he saw the black shape floating through the door into the room. He opened fire on it immediately. I swerved the falcon to the side and used the rest of the gas pellets to obscure vision in the room, then continued to fire and move, and fire and move, until all of its ammunition was depleted. Fortunately, as I had hoped, Paul also ran out of ammo in the deafening chaos of the fight. He was just a gun hobbyist, never in the military or even a peacer, so as I'd expected, he didn't count or preserve his rounds.

As Paul shook the empty guns in frustration, I quickly brought the bird back through the doors and into the elevator, and rode with it up to the roof, where I would have more room to maneuver for a last stand against the shielded man. As the elevator descended again to pick him up, I stood next to the aero and parked the falcon in the air on the other side of it, gripping my gun in my right hand and the remote in the other. When Paul appeared in the opening door of the elevator, I began firing repeatedly at him with the boa, as he instinctively turned his body and raised his left arm to cover his face. Now that he was out of ammunition unable to fire back, I was hoping that the close range might do some damage to the shield, and I also fired at parts of it that might possibly be weaker, like the feet, head, and the spot on his right hip where the "control pocket" was. But soon I was out of ammo myself, and Paul seemed unaffected by the bullets I had spent. Worse, when he stepped out of the elevator and straightened his body, I saw that he was holding another boa in his right hand, which he pointed at me.

"But you're out," I said with a sense of dread, when I saw his mocking smile.

"This is the gun you dropped earlier in the apartment," he said, savoring the expression on my face. "You forgot about it, huh? A big mistake for such a great war hero."

I dived for the shelter of the aero again before he stopped talking, but he still managed to hit me twice before I disappeared behind it. The desperate lunge managed to preserve my vital organs and arteries, but the bullets took chunks out of my left side and shoulder. Safe behind the car for now, I dropped the empty gun and passed the remote to my right hand. Then I sent the falcon crashing into Paul as hard as I could, which surprised him, causing him to stagger back a bit and fire wildly at it with his boa. He missed, fortunately, and I pulled the bird away and then farther back than it had been before, to produce more momentum. I sent it streaking at him again at full speed, but this time he was firing from a stationary position before it got to him, and he hit one of the wings twice. The falcon went spinning to the surface of the roof, bounced several times, and then lay motionless in a smoking heap. He fired several more times into it to make sure, which was *his* big mistake.

"Did you count your rounds?" I asked from my hiding place.

"No," he answered, looking at the gun, his brow knitted.

"I did," I said, took my glasses off, and stepped out from behind the aero.

He pulled the trigger several times in vain until he was sure the gun was empty, then he tossed it aside. We stood facing each other, and at the same time we both noticed the cluster of bullets hanging in the air on the left side of his chest, embedded in the shield. There were also others at various spots I had targeted. So Paul reached into the "pocket" on his right hip and pressed the control pad until the little wads of lead were catapulted away from him and clattered on the surface of the roof. He grunted in pain momentarily, before he reduced the shield's density, which showed that he wasn't wearing any body armor under the shield.

"I love that little trick, don't you?" he said.

"Give me the key to your aero and record a confession of everything you've done," I said, "and I may let you live."

"Oh, Michael, come on," he answered. "I know it wouldn't be a fair fight between us in a normal situation, you being the killer soldier and all." He spat this in disgust. "But you're wounded and wasted and I have the shield, which doesn't just protect me, like you've seen, but makes me stronger, too." The big man spread his shimmering arms wide. "Even if you could take me down, you'd be just adding to your horrible crimes and still be executed. Face it, I'm untouchable."

"We'll see," I said, and moved toward him.

I tried some normal attacks to the upper body, head, and legs to see if the shield had possibly been weakened or would allow slower objects in, but every place I hit or kicked felt like hardening cement and had no effect on Paul at all, except to make him laugh. Next, I got in closer, and in between dodging the arms that he was swinging wildly, I tried stopping my blows at the surface of the shield and pressing on it hard and slow, in case I could get inside it that way. But I couldn't, so I gave up and blocked one of his arm blows with both of mine, bruising them badly but allowing me to grab his arm with my left hand and use my right to find his fingers at the end of it. I figured that the shield had to open at that spot in order for him to hold the guns, and I was right. I worked some of my fingers between his and then bent his hand back like a game of "mercy."

Paul screamed in pain, and my idea was to subdue him in this way and force him to turn off the shield, or to do it myself while he was immobilized. But the big man proved more resilient than I had thought and used his free arm like a club to connect with my wounded left shoulder, and then my head. I lost my grip on his hand and staggered back so badly that I could barely remain standing. My ex-friend had been right again . . . the events of the last few days and my wounds had drained me to half the man I'd been before. So whatever else I was going to try, I had to do it now, while I still had anything left.

With no better idea coming to mind, I diverted Paul with some moves to his front, then maneuvered close to his side and used a takedown that would have been crippling in a normal fight. I dropped hard behind him, simultaneously clipping the back of his calves with both my legs and yanking on his arm until he toppled sideways onto the surface of the roof, which cracked and splintered at the impact. Unfortunately, the lower half of his body came down on mine, and the extra weight of the shield plus the "cement effect" made it my turn to scream out in pain. Paul, on the other hand, had only yelled in surprise, and soon managed to roll his body over onto my torso, which caused more screaming by me, and brought his free arm down on my face, which ended the screaming abruptly and left me barely conscious.

He started calling me every profane name he wasn't allowed to use around his parents, and pushed himself up by pressing on my chest, which by itself broke several of my ribs.

"I am so sick of you," he said, and using the extra strength he had from the antigravity field, he hauled my limp body up onto his shoulders and stalked to the closest edge of the roof. I knew there was an invisible barrier there, to provide some safety but not impair the view, but I also knew it was low enough that he could throw me over. I guess I had irritated him enough that merely crushing my skull wasn't a good enough death for me. And I was glad that I had, because as he was approaching the edge, I glanced down and saw the small control pad attached to his hip, inside the shield.

With a burst of renewed energy, I locked my left arm around the shield at Paul's neck, which I was able to do since it followed the basic contours of the human body. I jerked both legs down so that their weight pulled his head and upper body backward, which distracted him while my right hand searched for the opening to the controller pocket.

Paul started to thrash around in an attempt to shrug me off, but I held on long enough to get my hand inside the small hole in the shield. He must have felt me groping at the device attached to his belt, because his body suddenly froze when he looked down and saw my hand on it. Perhaps it took him a few moments to figure out what was going on, or maybe he was afraid of triggering the controls himself if he grabbed for my hand, so he didn't move at all except to swing his head sideways until our faces were separated only by the antigravity field of the transparent armor. Our eyes locked, mine narrowing and his growing wider as we both knew that whatever button my fingers found would either turn off the shield or increase its intensity. I hoped it would do the latter, because I had no fight left in me, and I was not disappointed.

Paul's dying scream lasted about a second, his larynx and every other bodily organ crushed from all sides concurrently. Since my eyes remained on his, I caught a brief glimpse of his head imploding before I was suddenly thrown more than five feet into the air, like I had bounced off a trampoline. I looked down at the top of my flight and was sure that I would come down on the other side of the barrier, beyond the edge of the roof, and fall to my death thirty stories below. But it turned out to be a sensory illusion, and I landed hard on the roof, next to Paul's barely recognizable body.

The man who would be king was now one ugly mess, to say the least. His skin that wasn't red from blood escaping was turning blue from blood being trapped inside, and his face looked like someone had painted it those colors and shrink-wrapped it by a process intended for something half its size.

But I wasn't much better off. As I lay still for a few moments, taking inventory of my injuries, I realized that at least one pool of blood was gathering slowly under my midsection, and the arm of my jacket was dripping red on the ground near it. Not to mention an assortment of broken bones. To my amazement, however, I could actually push myself up and stand. And I must have reached some kind of pain threshold, because it wasn't unbearable. Or maybe the pleasure I felt in my soul was canceling some of the agony in my body.

What had Kim called it in the bookstore? Being justified? Yeah, that was it. *Just-as-if-I'd* never done wrong, and *just-as-if-I'd* done everything right. And I thought of Saul—he had been vindicated, too. Perhaps this almost mythical cipher, whom I had desperately wanted to admire as the man of the century, really *was* after all—even with his faults. How unfair had I been to him, as so many others had, when in reality he carried more weight on his shoulders than most men would even have dared to bear?

I looked again at Paul's body in the dawning light on the roof, and I soon realized how bad this would all look when someone made his way up here—which probably wouldn't take long. Min himself would be returning soon, to find his master murdered by the guns I carried, and his son also dead at my hand. With no record of what had happened, and no witnesses to clear me, I would be pinned with the worst murder rap in history—if I even lived long enough to be arrested.

I could tell that I was dying; there was no question about it. And I wasn't even sure I would make it if I called security right now and turned myself in for medical attention. So there was only one thing to do: I had to find Lynn. I had to tell her that I was innocent. I had to tell her that I hadn't killed our daughter. I wanted to die in her arms.

I dug the glasses out, to find that by some miracle they

were still working. I dialed our home number, and prayed that she would be there, and that she would answer.

She did. And when I said her name, she hung up on me. But at least I knew where she was.

I reached into the pocket of Paul's shield again and lowered the intensity, trying to ignore the wet, gurgling sounds his body made as it decompressed. I searched through the bloody pockets until I found the key card for his aero, which I slipped into its door, hoping that my dead ex-friend had not activated all the security systems. He hadn't, and in no time I was in the sky over the bay, headed to the Napa Valley. The autopilot took me there, as I endeavored to plug my holes and stay alive a little longer by sheer force of will. I also prayed a few more times, since it had seemed to work before.

23

By the time our house was in view, I had leaked all over the interior of the aero. I was thinking it was good that the car wasn't mine, but then remembered that it didn't matter anyway, because I was just about gone. I kept telling myself, *Hold on, hold on*—but not verbally, because when I tried to speak, it felt like I was under water.

The car dropped and came to rest on the front driveway, close to the entrance because I didn't know how far I could make it. Lynn must have heard me land, because she opened the door before I could stagger to it.

"Oh my God!" she gasped, recoiling with horror at the sight of my blood-drenched and broken body, but then she rushed to me as I slumped to the sculpted stones that covered the ground. She knelt and hoisted my head and shoulders onto her lap, saying my name repeatedly when she saw that my eyes were closed.

I wasn't dead yet, though. I was merely attempting to gather enough strength to tell her what I needed to tell her.

I'm innocent, Lynn. I didn't kill our daughter. You were right—Paul lied to me. I'll be gone in a minute, but you must not remember me as a murderer, even though they'll say I was. I didn't kill Saul, either. Don't believe them when they tell you I did. Tell everyone that I was innocent. Stand by me. They might believe you . . .

But there was no way to say all this. The blood was even now trickling into my throat; soon it would rise and render me utterly mute. And that wasn't what I really needed to say, after all. There was something much more important, and more appropriate, which didn't require as much breath.

"Forghhh . . ." I choked on the fluid, and coughed up some of it. Then, with my throat clear for a couple of seconds, I got it out: "Forgive me."

Lynn wiped my lip and chin tenderly with her fingers, then seemed lost in thought for a moment.

"I don't know if I can, or even what that means," she finally said. She thought some more, then nodded her head.

"But I love you," she added.

I smiled, hoping to go out with one on my face, but then my clouding eyes mysteriously began to focus again, as if they were recognizing something before my mind had been informed. And after a few seconds of scanning the morning sky beyond Lynn's lovely head, they came to rest on a dark spot that seemed to be coming closer.

"What do you want me to do?" Lynn was saying. "Call a

medical team?" I shook my head no, then tried to focus on the dark spot again. It was now much bigger, so I could see that it was the oversized BASS aero that had been designed especially for Min.

I wondered why the estate's security system had not alerted us to his approach, but I didn't have time to worry about that. If the augmented man was coming to avenge Saul, he might also kill Lynn, as a part of the price I had to pay. Or perhaps Min had really been working for Paul all along. Either way, I didn't want to take any chances with my wife's life, so I nodded my head toward the advancing car and moved my hand like I was squeezing a trigger.

Lynn saw the aero and got the idea. She gently placed my head back down on the stones and ran into the house. By the time she came back out, carrying a big two-barreled Python revolver and an armored jacket, I had managed to roll onto my side, coughing up more blood as a result. She put the silver gun and jacket down next to us and situated my body so that I was sitting up, with her behind me. Then she spread the jacket across my torso to protect us, and handed me the gun. I held it with two hands and rested it on my lap, not wanting to spend the energy lifting it until I had to.

In silence we watched the aero float down toward us and land on the other side of the stones, about thirty feet away. It was pointed the other way, and the bald brown giant stepped out of it immediately and stood facing us. He was apparently unconcerned about my weapon, and I soon found out why.

I jerked the Python up and fired at him. The open door of

his aero, in front of which he had been standing, exploded in a shower of metal and glass. But Min had disappeared. Lynn extended her arm from behind me, pointing to the fountain in the middle of the driveway, which was on our right and closer to our position.

The big man crouched there, his one hand resting on the side of the little pool surrounding the fountain.

I fired again, and this time chunks of cement and water flew everywhere. But again Min had moved before the shells arrived. He flashed around Paul's aero to a spot behind us and, before I could even react, took the gun away from me. And then he stood in front of us, examining it with his huge hands as if it were a children's toy.

"We wouldn't want you to hurt someone," he said with a playful grin on his face. I had never before seen him speak or smile, and that was the last thing I saw.

The last thing I felt was Lynn's warm body against my cold back, her arms tight around my shoulders and chest, and her tears soft on my neck.

24

The memorial service was sad but beautiful, as the best of them are. It was at the grave site on a hill between the two higher ones that held the Ares house and Darien's. BASS had planned and publicized another service at the same time in the city, so that the press wouldn't find out about this one. They were probably already wondering, however, why nobody important was showing up in the city.

They were all here, of course. Most of the world leaders from the summit, and a few more who had not attended that night. A few close friends, from over the years, of the men who had died. And the mourning women—Liria Rabin, with her three children; the one who had mothered Darien's son, with another child who had been living with her; and Lynn, who had lost more than anyone. They all stood in a circle around the five simple yet elegant graves, their clothes and hair flapping in the midday mountain breezes.

A BASS chaplain, who had been cleared at the highest level of security, stepped from marker to marker, reading the epitaphs engraved on each. He started with Darien's, then his son's, then proceeded to Paul's, which was vague in the extreme. Saul Rabin's was lifted from William Blake:

In what distant deeps or skies
Burnt the fire of thine eyes?
On what wings dare he aspire?
What the hand dare seize the fire?

When the stars threw down their spears,
And watered heaven with their tears,
Did He smile His work to see?
Did He who made the lamb make thee?

And then it was time to remember Lynette, as the chaplain reached her marker. Lynn had wanted to leave it blank, so the eulogy consisted of a time of silence that stretched on and on, partly because the chaplain and all the guests wanted to show sympathy for Lynn.

Even more than that, however, they were rendering homage to the new chief executive officer of BASS, king of the Bay Area, and heir to the world.

I was sitting next to my wife, still healing from my wounds, in a wheelchair with no wheels. It floated several feet off the ground, powered by a small Sabon engine humming softly at its bottom. I imagined the bulky black seat to be a throne, as I surveyed the kind of men who were now bowing their heads before me. I glanced behind me at Min, who winked knowingly at his new boss, reminding me of the story he and Lynn had told me when I woke up.

My dear wife, who had thought Min had come to kill me, had been pleasantly surprised to find that he actually had come to *save* me. When she asked how he planned to treat a man whose heart was stopping, miles from a hospital, his reply was to pick me up and carry me into our garage, Lynn following close behind. The giant uncovered a hidden control box in one of the garage walls, and before the lady of the house could protest or question, the entire garage floor dropped down twenty feet, revealing a shiny new bank of underground elevators.

"Now that you know about this facility, we can rearrange the modes of access," Min had told her as they entered one of the elevators. "If you or Michael prefer something else."

All she could do was nod like a zombie, with her mouth hanging open, and say, "Okay."

A few seconds and four descending floors later, Min laid me down in a state-of-the-art operating room and went to work putting me back together, with an uncanny expertise in surgery and the best equipment BASS money could buy. The medical center, along with the rest of the underground base, was utterly deserted, but brand new and ready for use.

Saul Rabin had ordered it to be constructed in secret five years earlier, when his crews were ostensibly working only on my house and the one they built for Darien on a neighboring crest. The old man knew that the company would one day need to move its executive command somewhere other than the highly visible and potentially vulnerable castle in the city, and these deserted hills were ideal, for several reasons. It's amusing, in retrospect, because I'd always wondered why he secured the estates of the Napa Valley with such a tight air-defense system. The mansions and vineyards were certainly beautiful and valuable, but why would anyone want to attack them with jets or missiles?

Saul had also hoped that Darien and I would pass his rigorous tests and become the ones to inherit his kingdom, so he'd planned for us to live atop this impenetrable fortress, from which we could rule the Bay Area (and the world, if necessary). It filled the mountain underneath our house, stretched to the one underneath D's, and was replete with concealed hillside aero bays, communication and intelligence capabilities surpassing even those in the castle, and enough lab room to house all our classified research.

Of course, this was why the old man had not wanted us to visit the property while the house was being built.

"A *man* came up with this idea, right?" was all Lynn had said, concerned about how living on top of all this might affect the family that we planned to start anew. Min assured her, on behalf of Saul himself, that her life needed to be no different, and that she and hers would actually be safer here than anywhere else.

The big bodyguard could speak on behalf of Saul Rabin because Saul Rabin was inside him. Prior to the old man's death, much of his memories, knowledge, and experience had been transferred to the cyborg's neural capacitors (the wireless wetware in his brain). This was the end goal and result of Saul's Legacy Project, after he had rescued it from Paul's deviant designs and continued its development in secret. The old man had wanted his legendary leadership skills and irreplaceable life experience to be available for his successors, to assist us in the formidable challenges we would face. In this way he would live on beyond death, proving useful to generations yet unborn. According to Min, he could even *talk* to us by way of an artificial-intelligence construct—a rather morbid option that I wasn't yet ready to use.

I did, however, learn much from the memories Min now carried in his head.

I don't know if I'll ever understand all the old man's thinking and purposes, but here's what I could piece together: Saul had learned about Paul's Machiavellian schemes shortly after D's murder, and had let them run their course. He wanted to see if guilt and regret from committing such a horrible crime might possibly bring his son back to his senses, and he wanted to see if I was truly a capable replacement for both of them. So he tested me, first by allowing me to be victimized by Paul's lies, then by subjecting me to the pressure of the summit meeting, and finally by inviting me to the showdown with Paul in the penthouse. He could have skipped or stopped any of this, but he hadn't, because he'd been looking at the big picture of the future of his empire.

If Paul's lie had caused me to lose my composure completely, and I had killed myself or Saul, I would have proven that I was unsuited to be his heir. If I hadn't been able to overcome the obstacles placed before me that night, then Saul would have known that I didn't have what it takes to become one of the most influential and powerful men in the world.

On the other hand, if I triumphed against all odds, the old man would consider me a worthy successor. I had, and so he had. He had been pulling my strings and putting me through some unpleasant paces, but my feelings toward him were mixed because of the way it all turned out. In fact, now that I understood at least some of his plan, a degree of my former admiration for him had returned, plus a personal indebtedness for where he had taken me. At least I had to admit that Saul Rabin seemed to embody one of his favorite maxims, that the greatest men are the ones who make the most difficult choices. Or, as someone else once said, "Risk and destiny are synonyms."

One thing Min was not able (or willing?) to tell me, and which I looked forward to asking Saul's "ghost" when I felt ready to talk to it, was why he had chosen to groom *me* as an heir to his empire. I was far from the most intelligent or experienced candidate, so I sensed that there was something more to this than I was aware of at this point, something hinted at by his cryptic comment about my being the "true peacer."

But regardless of the reasons for the destiny that had been scripted for me, I was ready to embrace it, and really seemed to have no choice but to do so, in light of the epic resolution the old fox had engineered on my behalf. He had turned on the cameras in the penthouse and on the roof prior to our final confrontation with Paul, and everything they had recorded was routed to the cache in Min's head for safekeeping. So earlier today, Lynn and all the world leaders who came for the service were able to see, with their own eyes, Paul's confession and my subsequent heroics. Most important, they watched as every ounce of favor and respect that Saul Rabin had ever earned was transferred to me, when he willingly gave up his life to save mine.

Justification . . . just as if I'd never done anything wrong, and just as if I'd done everything right. And a promising future ahead—all because of what someone else had done for me. I now treasured this concept, because it felt as good as anything I had ever experienced.

As we were leaving the hill, Lynn's hand in mine, I looked back again at the row of graves, and was reminded of the pain it took to get me where I was. I had mourned them adequately, however, so now I took some comfort from the appropriateness of their final resting place. The Rabins, Darien, and the children were laid above a future home of BASS, symbolizing the fact that their lives and deaths, one way or another, had paved the way for the future. And though their passing from this world was the worst thing that had ever happened to me, I knew that it would somehow be a part of everything good that happened in the world to come.

All week the discordant notes of Mozart's *Hostias* and *Sanctus* had been playing in my head like a broken record. But today, for the first time, the sanguine strains of *Benedictus* were breaking through. It seemed that my soul was determined to finish the masterwork, like the ghostwriter of old, not willing to let it end with a sad refrain.

This day full of tears was the dying composer's last line.

But tomorrow full of hope is the one I want to add.

Acknowledgments

Many thanks to my editor, Brendan Deneen, who showed his good taste by believing in *Silhouette* and his great talent by partnering with me to make it a better book. And to Nathan and Calvin, who have done some of the same things for this project: I'm looking forward to your future!